"I'd have missed so much in life."

Wade went on to explain. "So many things—if I hadn't made it back. This for instance."

He pulled her around and against him. "A woman close to me again. I sorely missed a woman."

Miranda tried to move away, but he held her hard against him. "But you wouldn't understand a man's needs, would you, Miranda?" His voice had grown husky, his nostrils drawing in her delicate perfume. "You, who can put your fiancé to the back of your mind for a month, and then hesitate when I ask if you've missed him."

"Oh, but—" You don't understand, she'd been going to say, but she had to keep the secret of her false engagement. So much depended on it.

LILIAN PEAKE lives near the sea in England. Her first job was working for a mystery writer, employment that she says gave her an excellent insight into how an author functions. She went on to become a journalist and reported on the fashion world for a trade magazine. Later she took on an advice column, the writing of which contributed to her understanding of people's lives. Now she draws on her experiences and perception, not to mention a fertile imagination, to craft her many fine romances. She and her husband, a college principal, have three children.

Books by Lilian Peake

HARLEQUIN PRESENTS

HARLEQUIN ROMANCE

LILIAN PEAKE

climb every mountain

Harlequin Books

TORONTO • NEW YORK • LONDON
AMSTERDAM • PARIS • SYDNEY • HAMBURG
STOCKHOLM • ATHENS • TOKYO • MILAN

Harlequin Presents first edition November 1990
ISBN 0-373-11316-1

Original hardcover edition published in 1989
by Mills & Boon Limited

CHAPTER ONE

'I'M OFFERING you this position, Miss Palmer,' Felicity Faringdon declared, clasping her heavily ringed fingers and pressing her short back against the straightness of the upright chair she occupied, 'on one condition.' She surveyed the unadorned hands of the young woman seated on the opposite side of the marble fireplace. 'That there is in your life a young man whom you one day intend to marry.'

Answer no to that, the implication was, and this interview will end here and now. Miranda cleared her throat to give herself time to recover from the verbal bombshell that had just exploded at her feet. Taking a shaky breath, she began, 'I——' Another clearing of the throat. She had to think—and quickly.

She had wanted the job so much. Coming out of art college with excellent qualifications and the praise of her tutors ringing in her ears, she had hardly been able to believe how difficult it would prove finding the kind of work for which her qualifications suited her. She was, she eventually and disappointedly had to accept, one small, if talented, fish in an overcrowded sea.

Which was why the chance of this job, unconnected though it was with the world she had studied so hard to join, appealed to her so much. And now this! Could she perhaps invent a fiancé?

'I would wish, of course, to meet the young man,' Mrs Faringdon was saying, relentlessly driving home her point.

Which meant 'invention' was out. So, Miranda thought dejectedly, I might as well leave right now . . .

'I'm impressed with you, my dear,' Mrs Faringdon

was saying. 'Your appearance pleases me. Old-fashioned good looks, a healthy glow. None of the pallor of the world-weary young women I see all around me these days.'

Haltingly, Miranda thanked her for her compliments, her mind working overtime on the problem her now increasingly unlikely prospective employer had thrown down like a challenge.

'You may wonder,' Felicity Faringdon was saying, 'why I'm making this—I do realise—somewhat unusual condition.' She patted her expertly coiffured hair, her rings sparkling in the glow of the softly illuminated sitting-room.

The furniture was genuine antique; not a hint of 'reproduction' about it. The carpets spoke of wealth to walk upon should the owner so desire, the rich tapestry of the furnishings telling of money in the bank, if not to burn, then to keep her in comfort for the rest of her life.

'In a few weeks,' Mrs Faringdon was saying, 'when you've settled down in my house——'

She's speaking, Miranda thought, her mind still turning somersaults in its efforts to solve the problem, as if I've actually got the job!

'And,' Felicity Faringdon continued, 'have accustomed yourself to my routine, I intend to travel to Switzerland and live there for a while with you as my secretary-companion. I have a nephew, a freelance television reporter. He owns a chalet in Zermatt, and retreats there for peace and quiet whenever his somewhat formidable journalistic duties allow him to.'

Miranda nodded.

'His name—you might have heard of him,' Mrs Faringdon elaborated, her expression warming with pride, 'is Wade Bedford. The son of one of my sisters.' Her eyes did not waver from Miranda's astonished face. 'Ah, I see you're aware of his existence.'

Aware of his existence? Miranda thought, her heart

bounding. What woman in the country didn't know that that particular man lived and breathed? Her own heart-throb from the first moment she had seen him on the television screen—she had adored his image along with thousands of her own sex. And he was this lady's nephew?

'Women chase him incessantly,' his aunt was saying. 'They almost persecute the poor boy. Which is one of the reasons why he comes as often as he can to the fastness of his Swiss chalet. And, my dear,' pinning Miranda with her stare, 'I will not have it invaded by a young woman who has every intention of falling at his feet the moment he sets foot in the door.'

'I——' Miranda responded, shaking her head '—I've made a point, ever since I can remember, Mrs Faringdon, of never going with the herd.'

Did that get her out of having to produce a husband-to-be?

Felicity Faringdon's eyes crinkled. 'In some species, Miss Palmer, that could prove very dangerous indeed. Animals who deliberately separate themselves from their own kind do so at their peril.'

'What I meant was——' Miranda offered.

'What's his name?'

'I—I'm sorry?'

'This young man of yours—what do you call him?'

Non-existent, Miranda almost answered, really floundering now. 'It's——' she coughed behind her hand '—it's Thomas, Thomas Mansfield. He's my best friend Penny's brother.' Which was the truth, even if the act of claiming him as her fiancé was not.

'Ah, a good old-fashioned name. Not shortened, I hope? To Tom?'

'Absolutely not. If we do, he——' Pretends to thump us, Miranda almost added. 'He objects.' By the minute she felt herself drawn deeper into her web of falsehoods.

'And you love this young man?'

Miranda coughed again, nearly choking this time. 'Very—er—he's wonderful.' Had she managed to sidestep a direct, and quite untruthful, answer? It seemed she had.

'And of course he's handsome?' Mrs Faringdon's smile was indulgent.

'Well . . .' Miranda visualised Thomas's mop of red hair, his freckled face, his tall, sturdy figure, 'not really, but——'

'You think he is.' Mrs Faringdon's face expressed complete satisfaction. 'Tell him to give you his ring,' she added, 'otherwise other young men might get the wrong impression. Like thinking you're unattached and fancy-free. And available. And that,' with a swift, sideways glance at the portrait of her nephew which adorned the mantelshelf, 'would never do.'

'A ring? Well, Thomas is saving up for one, but he's——' Miranda moistened her lips '—he isn't finding it easy.'

'In that case,' Felicity Faringdon pronounced firmly, 'until he is in a suitable—er—financial position to provide you with the traditional token of his love, I shall lend you one.'

'You'll lend us a—a ring? That's very thoughtful of you, Mrs Faringdon, but really, we——'

'While I fetch it, will you kindly read through the notes I've just given you? If you can transcribe them without trouble, I shall be very pleased.'

Five minutes later she was back. 'You can understand my writing? Fine.' In her palm lay a ring, of modest design, but holding an old-fashioned charm.

'It has no sentimental value for me. I found it at the back of a drawer in a Victorian card-table I bought a few years ago. Here, try it on. No, no, third finger, *left* hand, Miranda. An excellent fit, and it looks charming. It's yours, my dear, until your young man is able to replace it with one of his own.'

That settled to her satisfaction, Mrs Faringdon asked, 'What's his job?'

The question shook Miranda. 'Job? You mean Thomas? He doesn't have one. You see, he's still a student.' Which at least was true. 'We got our diplomas at art college, but he decided to stay on and specialise. He's currently taking a course in photography.'

'Ah, so that ring will be entirely appropriate for a hard-up student to give to the girl he loves. So,' Mrs Faringdon's eyebrows lifted, 'marriage isn't even in the offing?'

'Certainly not! I mean,' hastily Miranda corrected herself, 'oh, no, not for a long time. We'll just have to be patient,' she finished with a flourish and a relieved smile.

'Before I give you my final answer, Miss Palmer, I shall want to see this fiancé of yours.'

Oh, heavens! Miranda thought, raking in her handbag. 'Somewhere in here there's a photograph——' Of Penny and herself, laughing at having been joined by a grinning Thomas who had just operated the delayed-action mechanism on his camera.

'Very nice, my dear,' said Mrs Faringdon, adjusting her spectacles. 'Heartwarming to see such happiness on your faces. And he looks a pleasant enough young man.' She handed back the picture. 'I shall look forward to meeting him.'

'Nothing I could say would make her change her mind!' Miranda exclaimed, as she sat on her friend Penny's bed in the Mansfield family home. 'She insists on meeting him. Oh, Penny,' Miranda clasped her long-fingered hands, 'what's Thomas going to say?'

'Well,' answered Penny, combing her long auburn hair and addressing her reflection, 'first, he'll fall about laughing. Then he might, just might, play ball.' She eyed her friend's bright, fair-skinned features, her oval-shaped face framed by silky, softly curling dark hair. 'He's got a soft spot for you, anyway.'

'But, Penny, if he's going to take it seriously . . . I mean, he isn't my fiancé, nor is he ever likely to be. All I want is for him to act as though he is when I take him to meet Mrs Faringdon. Just so that I can get the job—nothing else.'

Penny sighed, continuing with her grooming. 'Lucky you, even to have the chance of working for the aunt of Wade Bedford. He's fabulous! He should have been a film star, not a journalist. And you said he might even stay at the chalet while you're there?'

'It's a "hands off" policy all round, Penny, remember. If I so much as look at him in his aunt's presence, it's curtains for me. That's what she implied.'

'There's Thomas now, so let's go down and break the glad news.'

The new arrival was lounging in a chair watching television.

'Hi, brother,' said Penny, 'you lucky man. Meet your brand new fiancée.'

Thomas jumped up, then looked around furtively. 'Where? Tell me quick, then help me hide!'

'Right here.' Penny's head dipped towards their guest.

'You mean Miranda? She wouldn't look at me even if I offered her a fortune along with my handsome self. Would you, Miranda?'

'I—er—might, just might.'

Thomas's already pale skin seemed to turn even paler. Then he flushed scarlet. 'Are you *proposing* to me?'

'Stupid,' Penny reproached, 'it's not for real. It's—um—for business reasons, isn't it, Miranda.'

'Well, not exactly. It's your moral support I want, really. To help me get a job I want very much. You see, I need a fiancé.'

'You do?'

Miranda nodded. 'And to make it worse, my prospective employer won't take my word for it. I've got to produce a real live man, and the only one I could think of, apart from going up to someone in the street, was you.'

'Don't you mean *immoral* support?' queried Thomas, quirking a rust-coloured eyebrow. 'You're asking me to perjure myself in front of this man——'

'Lady—a rich one.'

'—lady?' Thomas did a double-take. 'And she's loaded? Ah, that could make a difference. Might she come up with a nice little cash payment for her employee when said employee was about to tie the knot?'

'Thomas, it would all be make-believe. Oh, forget it.'

'Be quiet, you two!' Penny was staring at the television. 'Miranda, he's on! Your heart-throb and mine—the nephew, *Wade Bedford*.'

Thomas stared at them both. 'So what? We've all seen him before. Hey, *whose nephew?*'

'Mrs Faringdon's,' his sister explained impatiently. 'Miranda's employer-to-be—that is, if you'll co-operate.'

'You mean she's *Wade Bedford's* aunt?' Thomas watched the screen wide-eyed. 'Hey, lead me to her! Any pathway to that guy, with his influence in the media——'

'You see,' Penny nudged a bemused Miranda, 'even young men put him on a pedestal. They want to copy him,' she said sagely. 'He's got what every man would love to have—sex appeal, brains, you name it. To women, he's just one big magnet, and what man wouldn't want to be that? I could watch him for hours!' she breathed.

'Wade Bedford reporting' flashed up on the screen as the journalist talked, raising his voice above the sounds of war around him. His tall, athletic figure, rising out of the dust and shimmering heat, made an immediate visual impact.

'Look at all those guns,' whispered Penny, her face pale. 'I'm sure he'll be——' She stuffed her fist into her mouth.

Like a theatrical backdrop—except that this was no film, this was for real—assorted weapons of war lay around the desert sand. Machine-guns spat out their deadly contents, while men in battledress crouched in the near distance, taking aim at an unseen enemy.

Against such odds, Miranda thought, he seemed so vulnerable. Her palms had grown moist, her heartbeats hammering. Wade Bedford faced the camera, his shirt open-necked, his dusty khaki trousers wrapping around his thighs in the strong, sand-laden breeze.

Each time an explosion shook the earth, Miranda and Penny jumped, but Wade Bedford did not even flinch. His eyes, like his hands, were steady and neutral. His tone was flat and unemotional, his words hitting targets within his listeners' brains, stirring their fears, yet at the same time their profoundest compassion. He held his audience spellbound.

'He's good,' Thomas declared. 'He's a great journalist. No one else could put it over like he does.'

'An expert manipulator of words,' Miranda put in, when the news item had ended. 'And that's not intended as a criticism. It's a fact.'

Penny agreed. 'I wanted to rush into the picture, shouting at them all to stop, then use their minds to work out a solution, instead of their hands.'

Thomas went to switch off the set, then stared at the blank screen. 'When my course is over, I could be out there with my camera, working with a guy like that.'

'Act the part of Miranda's fiancé,' said Penny with a wicked grin, 'and you might even be invited to go out there with *him*, with *Wade Bedford*.'

The idea plainly gripped him. 'It's a deal, pal.' He

held out his hand and Miranda grasped it. 'I'm your man.'

'Until I don't need you any more,' Miranda pointed out.

'Well, of course. Did you really think I meant for real? Married bliss isn't in the scenario I've written for myself. Well, not for years, anyway.'

'That's OK by Miranda,' Penny interposed, 'isn't it?'

Miranda nodded emphatically, her eyes shining at the thought that the job she wanted so much was within her reach at last.

Two weeks later Miranda leaned from the chalet window and filled her lungs with pure Swiss air. It was early evening and she should have been tired, with a flight followed by a long car journey behind her.

To her surprise, she still had energy enough for her eyes to devour the white surrounding beauty, for her sense of smell to appreciate the air's freshness and her ears to listen to the silence reaching down from the mountain peaks.

One of these drew her eyes constantly. Wrapped around with snow, it thrust high above the others, massive and commanding, pyramid-like almost, its smoothly eroded sides faceted by weather and numberless centuries. The Matterhorn, it was called, and Miranda stared with admiration tinged with awe at its fearsome remoteness.

From the floor above, she could hear Mrs Faringdon's self-assured voice speaking long-distance on the telephone. After meeting Thomas, she had confirmed Miranda's appointment as her personal assistant.

'I approve of him,' Mrs Faringdon had commented, 'in spite of his—er—slightly unkempt appearance. Other-worldly though you both are, with your artistic backgrounds, you should go well together.' Thus had her 'engagement' to Thomas received Mrs Faringdon's blessing.

Miranda had settled with reasonable ease into Mrs Faringdon's domain. The *objets d'art* with which she was surrounded gratified the artist in her. Her employer, she discovered to her pleasure, needed more than a secretary to type personal letters and reply to friends' correspondence. She also, it appeared, wrote articles for magazines, plus the occasional short story.

When Miranda's parents had heard about her coming trip abroad, they had been delighted. 'Aren't you glad,' her father had said, 'that you took that secretarial course which I suggested after you'd graduated from art college?'

Miranda had had to agree, despite the fact that, at the time, she had wrinkled her nose at the idea.

Prising her gaze from the view, she started unpacking her cases. The room was small and furnished simply, but with good taste.

Near the window was a table. This, her employer had told her, she could use as a desk. Somewhere, Miranda had also been told with a vague wave of the hand, she would find a typewriter—her nephew's, Mrs Faringdon said.

Three weeks had passed when Felicity Faringdon smiled in a kindly way. 'We get on well, you and I, Miranda,' she said. 'I hope I'm not working you too hard? This place seems to inspire me. The words start cascading out like——' she glanced outside, 'like an avalanche.'

So I've noticed, thought Miranda with a smile, secretly pleased that her employer had been able to supply her with so much work. Later that day, as they made their way to the dining area for their evening meal which Dorothea, the daily housekeeper, had prepared, the hall telephone rang.

Mrs Faringdon answered, joining Miranda at the

dining-table a few minutes later. Her face was pale, her hands uncharacteristically shaky.

'Bad news, I'm afraid,' she announced, lowering herself into a chair as if needing its support. 'That was my nephew.' She motioned to Miranda to pour some wine, her fingers closing tightly round the proffered glass. 'He's been wounded, badly enough to be forced to take sick leave. He was hit, he said, by a carelessly aimed spray of bullets.' She took a drink. 'It happened, apparently, while he was reporting to the camera.'

'Oh, how terrible!' Miranda exclaimed, her face paling, her artistic imagination picturing him sprawling helplessly, face down, on the rubble-strewn ground.

'He's restricted by his injuries, but reasonably mobile, and he's coming here to recuperate and convalesce. Hospital treatment and airline flights permitting, he'll be arriving, he says, in four days' time.'

CHAPTER TWO

ON THE DAY her nephew was due to arrive, Felicity Faringdon was surprisingly fidgety.

'I imagine he's on his way,' she murmured with a frown. 'I hope he'll be able to stand the journey without too much discomfort.'

Anxious or not, Miranda could not fail to notice that her employer did not allow the fact to interfere with her work schedule. Letters were dictated, ideas flowed from her seemingly tireless brain.

'Time to go!' she exclaimed at last on consulting her watch for the twentieth time. 'My nephew's train is due in fifteen minutes. Come with me, my dear, and meet the injured hero. Besides, I might want your help—suitcases and so on.'

She began to rise, when the telephone rang. 'Oh, not now!' she exclaimed, reaching out. A few moments later, her hand over the mouthpiece, she whispered, 'This call is important—from the USA. Unfortunately, it will take some time. Would you be good enough, Miranda, to meet my nephew yourself?'

Come face to face with the famous Wade Bedford, just like that? 'Oh, but—how will I recognise him, Mrs Faringdon?'

'You've seen him in action on the television news, surely? Tall, black hair, strong build.' From the street came the jingling of a bell. 'Oh, heavens, the taxi's here, right on time too. Off you go, there's a dear.' Mrs Faringdon watched Miranda pick up her bag and make for the door, then her apologies winged their cheerful way across the ocean to the North American continent.

The sensation of travelling in one of the little battery-

16

operated cars which roamed the streets, rather like a box on wheels, Miranda reflected, momentarily whisked her mind from the reason for her journey. The town was designated a traffic-free zone, which meant that petrol-driven vehicles were banned, leaving the air free of unpleasant fumes.

The taxi's mechanism whirred and Miranda dipped her head to look through the windows. Tourists strolled nonchalantly, spilling over from the pavements and into the taxi's path, hustling to one side when the driver jangled his bell.

As they neared the railway station, Miranda's apprehension increased. She was on her way, she reminded herself, to meet the man many women dreamed about. Not only that, a man who was almost a cult figure, famed for his reports from the world's trouble spots, admired as much for his bravery as his hard-hitting commentaries.

The station was quiet, surprisingly so, Miranda considered, in view of the imminent arrival of a train. One stood by the platform, but cleaners were busy working their way through its empty length. Puzzled, Miranda frowned at her watch. Had Mrs Faringdon made a mistake about the arrival time?

At the far end of the platform a lone figure stood, supported by a stick, a suitcase placed each side of him. Still not sure that this was the man she had come to meet, Miranda started walking. There was no doubt about it now. He was tall enough, compelling enough to be the man she had seen on the television screen. And—yes, she'd know him anywhere.

A few yards distant, Miranda halted. The man's cool gaze met hers, roving evaluatingly over her from top to toe. He seemed to be assessing her both physically and mentally, summing up her character, then placing her in his own private file under heaven knew what feminine category.

His gaze hit hers again and, try as she might, Miranda could not tear her eyes away. Inside herself she felt a leaping response, a silent reaching out. Her breath came unevenly and fast, like someone glimpsing a longed-for destination that was nearer than they'd thought. Then the image faded and she was back with a jolt to reality.

As far as this man was concerned, she was an engaged girl. Even if she were not wearing a ring, she knew he would not be interested in her. Remember, she admonished herself, all the women his aunt had referred to who had fallen at his feet. He had probably trampled all over them, then walked away. Mock engagement or no mock engagement, she wasn't going to be one of those.

'Mr—er—Bedford?' she enquired with a polite, if nervous, smile.

He inclined his head, eyes questioning.

'I'm Miranda Palmer, Mrs Faringdon's—I mean, your aunt's—personal assistant. She sends her apologies, but she's taking a long-distance call and——'

'Sent you instead.'

'Yes.'

'Mm.' He sounded doubtful, his eyes narrowing on to her features.

Did he really think, she wondered angrily, that she was going to embarrass him by being like all the other women Mrs Faringdon had mentioned so disparagingly? She had no intention of 'chasing' him, or 'persecuting' him, nor of 'falling at his feet'.

'Sorry I'm late, Mr Bedford,' she said with carefully assumed nonchalance, 'but your aunt must have——'

'The train was early. Let's go, shall we?'

There was a sudden weariness in his tone that brought all Miranda's tender feelings rushing forward. How could she have been so overwhelmed at meeting Wade Bedford, the celebrity, as to forget he was also Wade

Bedford, the man? The stars in her eyes had dazzled her vision so much that she had failed to detect the signs of strain and the deep fatigue of his whole bearing.

'You must be tired out,' she said, bending for his cases. 'I'm so sorry for forgetting. We'll find a taxi and——'

He stopped her in her tracks. 'I won't allow you to carry those.' He bent to take a case and winced.

'No, no, Mr Bedford, you really mustn't. Your injuries——' Her voice tailed off. Their eyes had locked in a strange kind of battle. Oh, no, she thought, that feeling—it's like walking into a dream world under the arch of a rainbow.

With this man in close proximity during the next few weeks, how on earth, she wondered with dismay, would she be able to behave as her employer would expect—as if no other man in the world except Thomas was worth a second glance? How could she control that uncontrollable yearning in the region of her heart every time she looked at him.

'I don't care,' he was saying, 'if your second name's Superwoman, you are not carrying my cases. Over there, there's a baggage trolley.'

Why hadn't she noticed for herself? She hefted his cases on to it, plus his airline bag. Watching, he had tensed as if his prime instinct had been to go to her—to any woman's aid. Pushing the load towards the station entrance, Miranda glanced back to check that he was following.

In doing so, she surprised a grimace of pain. For heaven's sake, she thought, how bad were his injuries? But his anguish was quickly hidden as, with the aid of his stick, he continued walking.

'Don't hurry,' she wanted to tell him, 'you'll only make the pain worse,' but already she had sensed the pride, the refusal to give in to any kind of disablement within himself. How else could he have stayed the course of his demanding calling?

Emerging from the station concourse, Wade Bedford turned briefly, looking upward, staring at the white, pyramidal shape of the Matterhorn as, swathed in wisps of evening mist, it towered above the town. You're like that mountain, thought Miranda with sudden insight, self-contained, enigmatic and utterly remote.

The chalet was a ten-minute taxi ride from the town centre. Wade Bedford stared at the passing scenery as if he were drawing it into him, as if it were a kind of medication, necessary to his return to full mobility and fitness.

His eyes dwelt lingeringly on the balconies massed with flowers, lifting to gaze at the chalets perched on the hillsides. The green slopes were patchworked with trees and dotted with huts for winter use, sheltering skiers and sheep alike from driving storms.

Disconcertingly, his gaze switched to Miranda. At once she looked away, attempting to hide from his perceptive eyes the high colour his action had provoked.

His hand on her wrist startled her head round. 'What——?' she began. His hold was firm, her skin springing to life beneath it.

'Who's the lucky man?'

Her ring had caught his eye. 'Man? Oh, you mean my——' The touch of him was making her pulse go crazy. 'My—er—fiancé? His name's Thomas, Thomas Mansfield.'

Watching that newsreel, Thomas had exclaimed, 'He's a great journalist. When my course is over, I could be out there with my camera, working with a man like that . . .'

Now was her chance to put in a good word for Thomas. 'He's a student,' she said, 'he's taking a course in photography. He—he'd . . .'

Horrified, she stopped. She had so nearly gone too far! He'd love to meet you, she'd been about to say.

Had she done so, the barriers would have shot up, and cynicism at her attempt to use him for her 'fiancé's' sake twisted those lips whose shape she found alarmingly pleasing.

An eyebrow lifted, his fingers releasing the wrist they had taken prisoner. Had he guessed the words she had so nearly uttered? Had he heard them many times before?

The taxi braked outside the chalet. Climbing out, Miranda turned instinctively to help her companion, but clasped her hands instead. He would surely have scorned her offer. Covertly watching him step out, she found herself wincing with him as for a few agonising seconds his leg, plainly the injured one, had taken his entire weight.

The driver unloaded the baggage while Wade Bedford found the necessary coins with which to pay him.

'Please let me carry your cases, Mr Bedford,' Miranda urged, but he gestured, asking the driver to carry them up the steps to the chalet's entrance.

Miranda ran ahead, pushing open the chalet door, standing back to allow the man to lift the cases inside. As he passed Wade Bedford, some money was pressed into his hand and he saluted his thanks, going on his way.

'Miss Palmer.' Wade had spoken through gritted teeth.

Turning swiftly, Miranda realised what his outstretched hand implied, and knew that such an admission of helplessness must have cost him dear. Then he seemed to realise just what he was asking of her and made a 'leave me' movement with his hand.

'No, no, I'll help you gladly,' Miranda declared and, pushing her arm through his, braced her muscles and assisted him up the few final steps. As she made to withdraw, he seemed to clasp her arm to his side and she felt the hardness of his frame. Something in her leapt, then subsided, and she released the breath which had somehow become trapped in her lungs.

'Wade, my dear boy!' Felicity Faringdon was there, full of compassionate welcome, her arms encompassing him. 'What have they done to you? You're so brave, and so foolhardy in the risks you take.' Releasing him, she looked him over, shaking her head, then led him into the living-room.

'It's the surge of adrenalin those risks provide me with that I thrive on, Aunt,' Wade responded with a faintly cynical smile, but Miranda was not fooled. She had glimpsed the gritted teeth beneath the taut lips. 'But it's good to be back.' He glanced through a window. 'Back to the sanity and peace of the mountains.'

With a deep weariness, he sank into a low chair and his eyes fluttered closed, but this was the only sign of physical discomfort that he permitted to break through his defences.

Felicity patted a sofa cushion and Miranda joined her.

'I was so sorry, Wade,' his aunt said, 'that I wasn't able to meet you, but I hope my very efficient young assistant——'

'Was very efficient in taking your place,' Wade broke in, smiling, although his eyes remained closed. 'I hope she'll last longer in your employment than the other young women who've come and gone.' His eyes came open, fixing on Miranda, making her heart leap.

'My aunt has this tendency, Miss Palmer,' he went on drily, 'to work all her personal assistants so hard that they walk out on her in no time, sojourn or no sojourn among the Swiss mountain scenery.'

'Wade, how could you let me down so?' his aunt protested, half laughing, half serious. 'I've discovered in Miranda someone who loves work as much as I do. She tells me she frets if there isn't enough to occupy her, isn't that so, my dear?'

Miranda nodded.

Sceptical eyes opened again, a quizzical eyebrow lifting, then he shut out the world once more. He was stretched fully out, hands clasped across his broad chest, the walking-stick he had been using propped against the chair.

'Have you told Miss Palmer——'

'Call her Miranda, Wade,' his aunt intercepted, 'for goodness' sake!'

'Only if she calls me Wade.' That compelling gaze was on her again. 'Say it, Miss Palmer.'

'I——' Call this man, idol of thousands, if not millions, of her own sex, by his first name? 'W-Wade.'

He inclined his head, eyes glinting. 'Miranda.' He was teasing her, pretending they had just been introduced.

'Told Miranda what, Wade?' his aunt enquired.

'The real reason for those other young women's abrupt departure from the scene?'

'Because one by one they fell at your feet the moment you set foot in the door,' Miranda supplied more than cynically into a faintly stunned silence. Wade stared narrow-eyed, then burst into laughter. His aunt looked uncomfortable and just a little reproachful.

'I admit I used those words, Miranda, at the time of your interview, but I never intended you to repeat them within my nephew's hearing.'

'It's OK, Aunt, I'm not entirely unaware of the peculiar effect I seem to have on the opposite sex.'

'Well, Mr Bedford——'

'Wade,' he corrected with a mocking smile.

Miranda let out a short, indignant breath. '*Wade*,' she said, teeth gritted, face flushed, 'there is absolutely no need for you to worry about having that "peculiar effect" on *this* member of the opposite sex. First,' she counted on her fingers, 'as I told Mrs Faringdon from the start, I never follow the herd. Second, I would never, ever fall at any man's feet. And third, I have a man of my own, remember?' She flashed her ring, never dreaming that her 'engagement' to Thomas would prove such a useful weapon in putting the famous Wade Bedford in his place.

Wade, unmoved, looked at her steadily.

'So have no fear, Mr—I mean, Wade, I shall never lose my heart to you, no matter how many women might have done so in the course of your scintillating career.' She rose quickly, before her rapid breathing showed. 'Please excuse me, Mrs Faringdon. You must have lots to talk about to your nephew. If you need me, I'll be in my room.'

Miranda sank on to the bed, calming herself, arms clasped around her as if she were in pain. Did I have to tell such a lie? she asked herself. Three lies, in fact, because I'm not engaged, nor have I got a man of my own. Also, Wade Bedford is every bit as attractive and has just as devastating an effect on a woman's emotions as I thought he might have. *And he's had an absolutely soul-shattering effect on mine.*

Going to the table which served as a desk, she pushed aside the typewriter and tugged free a sheet of cartridge paper. The tools of her artistic trade were never far away, since the urge to put pencil to sketchpad seemed to be overtaking her constantly in the beautiful surroundings in which she found herself.

On to the paper she almost threw a likeness of Wade Bedford, filling in the outline, broad and lean, hands in pockets, shading in the background of war and violence. Then she turned to the features of the world-renowned journalist, and the similarity to the actual man came through so strongly from her angry fingers that, as she leaned back and surveyed her work, a gasp escaped her.

She lifted the pencil and ran a cross through the entire sketch. As she threw the pencil down, the eyes—Wade's eyes—seemed to blaze with an unrestrained fury. Then it was gone, and the expression in them became an enigmatic, deeply disturbing stare.

'Something wrong, Mr Bedford?' Miranda asked anxiously, watching Wade's recumbent form.

Dinner was over, and Felicity had left them with the request that, in her absence, Miranda should keep their visitor company. Since which time the telephone had alternately pinged and rung as the lady, in her office on the topmost floor, had either made or answered overseas calls. Plainly the cost of such activity, which she apparently thoroughly enjoyed, did not concern her one atom.

The man in question did not stir, stretched out as he was in the low chair as if that were the only position he had discovered which relieved his physical discomfort. His eyes were firmly closed, but Miranda sensed that he was anything but at ease.

'Wade?' It was almost a whisper, but her use of his first name elicited a response—the faintest movement of his shoulders, the slightest of shrugs.

'Are you,' she ventured, 'are you back in the war zone, surrounded by furious men with guns and hand-grenades?'

The grey eyes came open, their expression unfathomable. 'What does our sweet young Miss Palmer know of such things?'

His faintly sarcastic tone did not annoy her. He had been through so much, he probably held a jaundiced view of everything, let alone the comings and goings of his aunt's personal assistants.

'Only what I see on television. When it all spills out into the viewers' living-rooms, it's so frightening, they're almost living it themselves, aren't they? Don't think it doesn't bite deep into their very depths.'

'You're implying it makes them want to reach for the

alcohol, or alternatively, their tranquillisers?'

'I am. It's bad enough when you're sitting safely in an armchair. What it must be like to do what you do, to be in the thick of all that carnage . . .'

'Don't bother even trying to imagine, Miranda. There's damn all any of us can do about it, whether we're merely watching it happen, or surrounded by it all, reporting it to the world. Is it possible, do you think, to——' He went through the motions of rising, then fell back, head resting. 'Forget that.'

'Help you? Of course I can.' Gone was her anger with him for being so macho earlier about his own attractions for women. She had vented it, hadn't she, in the act of drawing him, then eliminating him from her feelings with the furious crossing out?

'Softness of heart—from one of my aunt's assistants? It was almost worth getting injured for—just to see that look in your eyes.'

His strong mouth widened into a lazy smile and her heart took it upon itself to cartwheel around her chest. She hadn't eliminated him, after all; his magnetism still made her legs go weak.

His whole face had been transformed by the smile, throwing off the years which had been added by his recent gruelling experiences. Oh, dear, Miranda thought, near to despair, there's that irresistible something about him again! It was potent, intoxicating and dangerous, and made her sensual responses do a crazy jig.

Did he *know* what he was doing to her? His grey eyes flashed. There seemed to be a message in them so powerful that she almost went to him as if drawn by a magnet. *Was he trying to make her forget her vow never to fall at his feet?*

'Miranda.' Her name drifted whisper-soft across the room. His hand came out. 'Will you help me?'

Despite the danger of giving in to that magnetism—it

could lose her her job, couldn't it?—it was a question that touched her compassion, which was but a short step to her heart. Was he perceptive enough to know that? But she didn't even want to try to resist, wanting instead to run to him and shield him from any misfortune that life might throw at him . . .

He started to ease forward and she moved swiftly to his side. One of her arms went across his back, the other under his armpit. With great caution, he shifted his injured leg, which had been stretched out, into position for use. As Miranda began to lever him upward, his muscles tensed and she felt his ribs jerk with a sharp indrawn breath.

Half lifting him, she grew conscious of the hard, fast beat of her heart. It was the effort, she told herself, it was nothing to do with the way he felt in her arms, the bones of his ribs expanding and contracting against the softness of her breasts as he allowed his body, for a few fleeting moments, to rest against hers.

'Your fiancé,' he observed, 'is a lucky man.'

Miranda looked into his face, searching for the cynicism that was not there. All the same, he hadn't meant it. He was pale and washed out, the effort of rising seeming to have temporarily exhausted him, and the cliché had been his way of thanking her for her help.

'Miranda, what——?' Felicity Faringdon stood in the doorway, her face forbidding.

'It's not what it seems, Aunt,' Wade said wearily. 'I have no plans to seduce your valued assistant. And the way I feel, even if I had, I can assure you . . .' A slow shake of the head completed the sentence.

'Wade needed my support, Mrs Faringdon,' Miranda broke in hastily.

'All you needed to do, Wade,' Felicity said, 'was to say the word and I'd have come at once. Now, where are you making for? Let me take over, Miranda.'

'With your permission, Aunt Felicity, and with no

disrespect to you, I'd rather your strong and somewhat more youthful assistant helped me upstairs.'

'You're making me feel my age, young man,' Felicity scolded with a smile.

'I didn't intend to, Aunt. The point is that I can allow her to take more of my weight than I could you. That is, if she's willing?' He regarded Miranda, eyebrows raised. His aunt could not see, as Miranda could, the challenge in his look.

'I——' For some reason, Miranda's voice had become husky. 'I'm willing.' The words sounded a reverberating echo somewhere in her brain, implying so much more than had been intended.

'Right.' They were at the foot of the stairs, Miranda's supporting arms round Wade's waist. For a few moments they stood thus and, close as she was to his chest, she could hear the pounding of his heart and the jerk of his breath. He was feeling the effort, no doubt about that, his breathing uneven through pain.

Bending, she put her hands on each side of Wade's waist. There was sinew there and a hard spareness of flesh, not a single pinch of surplus layers. Reaching the wide landing at the top of the staircase, Wade indicated the room which lay on the other side of Miranda's. This, she recalled, was where she had found the typewriter, the room which, she had sensed at the time, had an air of waiting about it.

The occupant, without whom the room had seemed so large, pulled himself into its centre and filled it to its corners with his presence.

Glancing at him, Miranda saw that he had closed his eyes. Remaining silent, she almost felt the relief and thankfulness that wrapped around him, and it was as if she were gazing all over again at the Matterhorn, encircled by evening mists and retreating into its own remote and impregnable eyrie.

CHAPTER THREE

FOR four days, Wade did not surface. He was resting, his aunt explained, on doctor's orders. Miranda would not admit to herself that she missed him, that his absence was as potent to her emotions as his presence.

One morning the sun, shining as it often did, straight into her eyes, woke her up. Glancing at her watch, she discovered that it was barely six o'clock, yet the aroma of coffee drifted upward from the kitchen.

The housekeeper did not usually arrive until seven-thirty, which could only mean that her employer was up and about and wanting to work, unusual though it was. Normally, Mrs Faringdon liked to have most of her mornings to herself. This was why she sometimes asked Miranda to work later in the day, to enable her to catch up with her letter or article writing.

Hurrying to the bathroom, Miranda took a quick shower. Her employer became a bit jumpy if she was kept waiting, especially if her mind was alive with original thoughts and working overtime.

And, Miranda reasoned, since hers was a job she had grown to like very much, even though it offered her no chance of utilising her artistic ability, she considered it a good idea to pander to her employer's whims. If getting up unexpectedly early was one of them, then she had no quarrel with that.

From the rail on which her clothes hung, she chose a low-necked blue cotton shirt, teaming it with a flower-patterned skirt. Running the comb through her dark hair and hearing it crackle with life, she raced down the stairs and made for the kitchen.

'Mrs Faringdon,' she exclaimed breathlessly. 'I'm

sorry I'm late, but——'

No sign of the aunt, but the nephew was there. The coffee machine bubbled away as if enjoying a private joke.

Miranda stopped short, Wade's sudden appearance after four blank days robbing her of speech and sending her blood swirling through her veins.

Arms folded, he leaned back against the stainless-steel sink. His pitch-black hair looked as if it had not been combed after a shower, his jaws and cheeks boasting a night or two's growth of beard, while his mouth flirted with a faintly mocking smile.

'H-hi!' Miranda exclaimed, for want of something better to say.

He inclined his head, his smile now faintly cynical. 'What a welcome! Did you mistake me for your fiancé—Tom, did you say his name was?'

'Thomas. Mansfield,' she added, more for Thomas's sake than anything. 'And no, I didn't think you were him.'

'He.'

She frowned, then realised, smiling. 'Please excuse my grammatical error. I should have remembered I was talking to a celebrated journalist.'

'One day,' said Wade, eyes darkening, 'your impudence will get you into trouble.'

'Sorry.' She smiled widely, not sorry at all. How could she be when her heart was dancing on tiptoe at the sight and proximity of this screen idol in her line of vision? 'How are you feeling?'

'Better, thanks. The doctor was encouraging. Rest, he advised, and help Nature carry out the healing process. So I rested. And slept.'

She nodded, comprehending.

Despite his semi-invalid state, all the fatigue he had displayed four days ago seemed to have vanished. His eyes were quick and sharp, windows on a brain cleared for action.

More than ever, Miranda was aware of his height and athletic bearing. As he stood unsupported, his stick hooked over the back of a chair, she saw him as he really was—a tall, tough-minded man, broad-shouldered and, injuries apart, in superb physical form.

He looked at her with a half-smile, his appraisal of her distinctly feminine shape uninhibited and sensual. That femininity in her was responding at full power, and there seemed to be no way she knew of switching it off.

His good looks, laced with a deep intelligence, gave a strange twist to her insides and played havoc with her equilibrium. He was causing such an upheaval in her own private world, it was as if all her emotions were caught in some internal centrifugal force, spinning uncontrollably.

'Your—your hair's wet,' she remarked, filling the silence. 'How did you manage to shower without help?'

'I didn't. I can't even take a bath at the moment. I had an all-over wash.'

'Oh.'

'Would my life-support machine have helped me shower if I'd attempted it?' There was a wicked gleam in his eye at her embarrassed flush.

'If you mean me, my willingness to help people doesn't stretch to assisting naked men take showers.'

He laughed, eyes lighting up, face transformed, pain lines smoothed away. 'The images that statement conjures up bring even my world-weary body to life!' He sobered and his gaze wandered over her. Could he read everyone, Miranda wondered, as minutely as he seemed to be reading her?

'Your fiancé excepted, of course.'

'You mean—do I help *him* take a shower?' She coloured furiously. 'Of course not!' Confused by his frowning scrutiny, she turned away. 'I thought you were

Mrs Faringdon. Which is why I hurried down.'

'So the welcome was meant for her?' An eyebrow twitched.

'It was an apology, really. I thought I was late.' That didn't, of course, explain the brightness in her eyes as she realised that it was her employer's nephew she was greeting, so she added, 'It was for the beautiful morning, the wonderful world out there just waiting to be explored.'

Indicating a cup, she asked, 'Coffee for you? Milk, sugar?' He refused them both, and she watched as he sat painfully at the table, restraining her impulse to help.

The kitchen fitments were of varnished wood, the higher cupboards glass-fronted. There was a rustic feel to the room, despite the modern equipment.

'This chalet,' Miranda commented, looking around, 'must have cost you a lot of money.'

'It wasn't cheap.'

She nodded. In estate agents' windows in the town, she had seen such places advertised for breathtaking sums, price-graded according to size, and this chalet was certainly no rabbit hutch.

'By the way, my typewriter's missing.'

Miranda shifted uncomfortably. 'I've been using it. Your aunt——'

'Gave you permission in my absence. So what if I need it?'

'I don't know.' She frowned. 'Mrs Faringdon will probably have to buy one. But,' she looked at him doubtfully, 'you're supposed to be resting, aren't you, not working?'

Wade shrugged. 'I've had letters, requests from various sections of the world's media—you know the sort?'

'Interviews, articles, voice-over commentaries on the areas of conflict you've been reporting on? Even being invited to present television programmes?'

He looked at her sharply. 'What do you know about such things?'

'Very little, really. They were intelligent guesses.'

More accurately, in the course of her art studies, they had touched on such matters, but Miranda was not going to tell him that. She did not want to risk his derisory comments on her achievements.

'With the emphasis on "intelligent",' Wade was saying. 'My aunt's surely hit the jackpot this time—a personal assistant with intellect, not to mention brains.' His eyes skated over her. 'In addition to good looks.' He paused. 'When did you last see your fiancé?'

The question startled her. 'I—um—let me see.' She made a play of counting. 'Nearly four weeks ago, just before we came over here.'

'Do you miss him?'

'Well, I—I suppose I do. Why,' she asked, quickly changing the subject, 'did you get up so early this morning? Especially when you were supposed to be taking it easy.'

His brilliant eyes dazzled her. 'Maybe, like you, I couldn't resist the call of the morning sun?' He began to lift himself out of his chair. Following her instinct, Miranda's arm came out, providing support.

His gritting teeth told of pain determinedly suppressed, but he straightened and, before she could put a distance between them, his arm had found its way around her waist. He pulled her closer and she became completely still. Not by a single movement must she betray how he made her feel. Her breath came faster as his hand pressed against the side of her head, guiding it slowly but firmly, so that her cheek came to rest on his ribs.

'Hear my heartbeats, Miranda?' he asked. 'Are they loud and clear?'

'Going like a hammer in a hurry,' she whispered.

A cut-off sigh escaped him. 'They very nearly

stopped.' She flinched, but he held her still. 'There have
been times, Miranda, in the course of my work, when
I've wondered if I'd come through the day alive.'

Shakily, she inhaled his musky scent and, to her
dismay, experienced an instant firing of her desires, her
femininity stirring to demanding life, sweeping her with
a longing to merge and melt into his powerful
masculinity.

'And when,' he went on, 'miraculously, I did survive,
in the night I'd feel the shock of the day's events
catching up with me. I knew that if I hadn't made it, I'd
have missed so much in life. So many things . . . This,
for instance.' He pulled her round and against him so
that her breasts became imprisoned beneath the rigidity
of his chest. 'A woman close to me again. I sorely
missed a woman.' She tried to move away, but he held
her hard against him. 'But you wouldn't understand a
man's needs, would you, Miranda,' his voice had grown
husky, his nostrils drawing in her delicate perfume,
'you, who can put your fiancé to the back of your mind
for a month, and then hesitate when I ask if you've
missed him?'

'Oh, but——' you don't understand, she had been
going to say, but she had to keep the secret of her false
engagement. So much depended on it. The pressure of
his head against her breasts was agitating her, and she
had the greatest difficulty in keeping her hand from
stroking his hair.

'You wouldn't comprehend a man's aching longing
for his partner, his lover. You,' he drew in the scent of
her again, 'a woman like you.'

Unable to stand it any longer, she tugged free, staring
at him, her breasts still throbbing even though the
pressure of him had gone.

'I'm engaged,' she exclaimed agitatedly, 'and you
know it!' She extended her left hand with its ring, but
even that small item of jewellery, she reminded herself,

told a lie all its own. 'I'm marrying Thomas Mansfield.' As she uttered the untruth, her fingers crossed at her side, and she hoped that his normally acute perception might be dulled by his injured state.

It was as though a safety curtain had made an unscheduled descent during a stage performance. Wade's features donned an impenetrable mask, all emotion wiped away.

Miranda fled, hearing the outer door open and Dorothea's accented voice greeting the chalet's owner.

It was evening before she saw Wade again, all of her day having been spent with Mrs Faringdon, working flat out, her employer had laughingly said, in an almost impossible effort to keep up with the breakneck speed of her brain.

At dinner, Wade acknowledged her politely, speaking for much of the time to his aunt. As soon as she could, Miranda escaped to her room, staring from the window and wondering for how long after his convalescence Wade would remain at the chalet.

The sooner he left, she reasoned, the sooner her world would return to normal, and she would regain her emotional balance. While, in theory, there was no impediment to her falling headlong for Wade Bedford—and she could no longer fool herself that he meant nothing to her—in reality, for the sake of her job, if nothing else, the pretence that she had willingly taken on board that her heart belonged solely to one Thomas Mansfield must persist.

Sighing, she turned from the window, only to jump violently at the sound of a rap on the door. About to invite Mrs Faringdon in, she saw the handle turn, the door swing open, to reveal the tall figure of Wade Bedford filling the doorway. His head was high, despite the slight sagging of his shoulders and the drawn look around his eyes.

With a 'May I?' that was more a statement of intent

than a request for permission to enter, he came into the room, his stick supporting his slow movements.

Miranda, robbed of speech by the unexpectedness of his arrival, nodded and moved to help. He waved her gesture away and looked around him. With raised brows and a mocking smile, he queried, 'Why do I get the impression that this room's a battlefield and that you're my enemy?'

About to deny his assertion, she produced a smile, looking round also. 'I know it's not exactly tidy, but it surely isn't that bad. And,' she couldn't resist adding, 'I'm friend, not foe.'

'You could have fooled me.' He made for the desk and with another 'May I?' that wasn't a question, eased himself into the swivel chair. His gaze moved over the layers of paper and files which formed imperfect heaps that were just this side of chaos.

'Does my aunt know,' he shot at her, frowning, 'what an untidy, unmethodical secretary she's got? What are your qualifications?'

If he but knew it, very few. Miranda prepared to defend herself, but decided to try to turn the awkward moment into a joke. 'You've found me out! Are you going to persuade Mrs Faringdon to sack me?'

'I dislike impostors.' His words were clipped and deadly serious, and a stab of fear made her give a soundless gasp. 'How the hell did you get this job?' His cold eyes found hers. 'If my aunt had been masculine, I'd have said on looks. Since she's most definitely not, then how did you get round her?'

'I don't know what you're implying, Mr Bedford,' Miranda blazed, 'but whatever it is, I resent it! When Mrs Faringdon interviewed me, I told her the truth about my work experience and qualifications.'

'Which are?'

'Why don't you ask her? She's the one with my *curriculum vitae* filed away.'

'I'm asking you——' He paused, staring at the desk. His hand shot out, grasping the corner of a sheet of paper, sliding it from underneath a pile.

'No, no!' Miranda gasped. 'That's mine, that's private . . .'

She was too late. Wade gazed at the sketch of himself surrounded by tanks and guns and destruction. It was the one she had drawn on the evening of his arrival, and in an outburst of anger against him—and against herself for wanting the impossible, in the shape of Wade Bedford—had scored through the entire portrait.

'Whose work is this?' Expression inscrutable, his eyes seemed to pierce through to her very soul. There was really no doubt because, in a final act of defiance, she had scrawled her initials across the corner.

She pointed to them. 'Mine. I——' she had to clear her throat, 'I'm sorry, but——'

'But what?' There was silence for a few minutes as he stared at the portrait, saying at last, 'You hate me that much?' His finger indicated the giant crossing out of his face and figure.

'I don't hate you at all. I——' Just wanted to get you out of my hair, my mind, my life . . . How could she tell him those things?

She grasped the telltale drawing, trying without success to erase the cancelling lines. Seizing another chair, she moved it to the desk, seated herself in it and turned over the piece of cartridge paper.

With lightning-fast movements, she produced another sketch of him. Even as she worked, the essence of him came through—his humanity and compassion, his hatred of conflict, his courage in the face of danger. Miranda gazed at her effort, hardly believing that the portrait had come from her own hands.

Then she pushed it in front of him. 'Now accuse me of hating you,' she said thickly.

For some time he looked at her in-depth

interpretation of his character, then turned the chair slowly, and just a little painfully, towards her. 'Where did you train?'

She named the college. 'I—couldn't find work in my chosen line. In the end, I'd have taken anything, but as I discovered, so would many others with similar qualifications to mine.'

'Which is how you came to be employed by my aunt?'

He had put her on the defensive. 'She knows about my background, so I'm not one of those "impostors" you say you hate.'

But aren't I? she asked herself. What about my mock engagement, the things I said about never falling for a man like him?

Wade glanced at the portraits again. 'You're wasted here.'

'If that's a compliment, then thanks, but I like this job. I don't want to lose it. I'll——' she looked at the untidy layers on the desk, 'I'll improve at the secretary game. I'll tidy this lot up. I'm not entirely without training in office work—I took a secretarial course. Anyway,' she shot him an angry look, 'I don't see why I should defend my actions to you. You're not my employer.' The annoyance in his face could not be mistaken. 'I'm sorry,' she said again, 'but——'

'It irks you that you're having to play typist to a middle-aged lady, when you could be using your talent—and,' Wade glanced at the drawing in his hands, 'make no mistake, you are talented—to get to the top?'

'Thanks for the flattery——'

'I don't chuck flattery around. It was the truth.'

Miranda lifted a shoulder. 'All the same, I like working for your aunt. She pays well. I'm saving up——'

'For your wedding?'

The question winded her. She had forgotten her role! 'That's a long way ahead. Thomas is still a student.

He's full of ambition, has great plans for his future career.' In collaboration with you, she thought, if you but knew it.

'That makes two of you—both pulling, no doubt, in opposite directions. Don't you think you might have been too hasty in linking your life so irrevocably to his?'

How to answer that? she wondered worriedly. 'No, I——' Had to, to get this job, to earn some money, to repay my parents who were so generous to me while I studied, and who still support me financially if and when I need help. 'I don't think so.'

She held out her hand for the drawing, but he proceeded to roll it carefully. 'Mine, I think, since it's of me.'

About to protest, she decided against it, secretly flattered that such a man as Wade Bedford should want to keep any of her work.

With the aid of his stick, he reached the door. 'Since it appears from what you say,' he remarked casually, 'that you've both got your careers in front of you, why don't you say to hell with convention and simply live together?' He made to go, but turned back. 'It's the modern way, or so I'm told. Speaking personally, I've fought shy of emotional involvement. That way, there's been no tearful woman constantly begging me to give it all up and return to the fold.'

His cynicism hit Miranda hard. 'How can you dismiss man and woman relationships as if they're irrelevant and meaningless?'

'You think that staying free of involvement makes me callous and without feeling? Don't confuse freedom from ties, Miranda, with an absence of warmth. I could become very—er—warm.' His hard eyes skated over her and she could have sworn that in his imagination he was undressing her. 'With the right woman.'

As the door closed on him, her hands flew to her burning cheeks. He was arrogant and overbearing, and she would waste no more of her time thinking about him.

The trouble was, she sighed, going to the desk and sorting in a desultory way through the correspondence spread across its surface, that he kept inviting himself into her mind in the same way as he had omitted fifteen minutes ago to gain her permission before entering the room.

CHAPTER FOUR

'MIRANDA, my dear,' Mrs Faringdon murmured across her desk as her assistant waited patiently, notepad and pencil in hand, 'you're wasted here, utterly and completely.'

Miranda's heart sank. No need to ask her employer what she meant. She had used her nephew's words, which meant that they must have discussed her. What was coming now? she wondered. A gentle hint that she should leave, that, since all her qualifications were in another field, her experience in secretarial matters was just not good enough?

'He showed me that drawing you made of him, and my dear, it wasn't just good, it was excellent.'

'But it only took me a few minutes!'

'Nevertheless, you caught something elusive, looked into his depths, found his essence. Given the chance, Miranda, you'd go far in your chosen line.'

Her assistant swallowed convulsively. 'But, Mrs Faringdon——'

'Miranda,' Felicity said gently, 'I know a great many people. I have dozens of contacts in the media. I could almost certainly get you a——'

'It's very kind of you, but I don't want another job. I've got this one. I enjoy working for you.' Miranda's voice had risen in her effort to convince her employer.

Felicity smiled, patting the air as if to calm it. 'Say no more. If that is your wish, I certainly won't be the one to upset the status quo.'

Implying, Miranda wondered, reassured by Felicity's words, that, given half a chance, her nephew might? That because she hadn't fallen flat on her face offering him her undying love, his pride had been wounded so deeply, he had become determined to get her thrown out of her job as his aunt's assistant?

But, she thought in some puzzlement, he had not struck her as possessing any personal vanity at all. And as for falling for him, she reflected with a silent sigh, heartwhole she was definitely not, and it wasn't a young man called Thomas she had metaphorically given any portion of that organ of her body to . . .

The doctor called that day. He had dressed Wade's wounds, Felicity informed her, telling him that, since his progress was good, he would send a nurse in future in his place.

They were drinking after-lunch coffee in the living area when Wade told his aunt, 'The doctor advised me to take a walk now and then to exercise my limbs.'

'But, Wade, dear, you can't go out alone, not at your present stage of recovery!'

'Would you come with me, then?' A smile lurked in Wade's voice as he anticipated Felicity's refusal.

'Oh, I'd like to, Wade, if only I had the time. As you probably know, I take my exercise in small doses. I realise that's not a good thing to do, but as you've probably noticed, my work occupies so much of my time.'

Wade thought for a few moments, his half-smile persisting. 'Would you allow your secretary to hold my hand?'

'You mean accompany you? Now, Wade, you know I——'

'Yes, I'm aware you don't want to lose her through your nephew's Machiavellian intentions, but I assure you, Aunt, I was speaking figuratively. All I need is for her to walk by my side, mainly for safety's sake.'

His aunt sighed resignedly.

'So you'll lend her to me now and then, until I can walk alone?'

Which, thought Miranda, studying her tightly
interlaced fingers, was surely what he had every
intention of doing all his life?

'I'll be trusting you, Wade . . .'

He laughed. 'Oh, yes, you can trust me, Aunt.
Besides, the lady in question is already spoken for, as
they used to say.' A satiric glance was turned in
Miranda's direction. 'Would your beloved object?'

'To my walking out with you?' She smiled widely,
well aware that the words had possessed, in the past, a
more romantic connotation.

His lips firmed at her provocation, but he did not take
up the challenge.

'No,' Miranda assured him, and with truth, although
her listeners were not to know that, 'Thomas wouldn't
mind.'

'That's settled, then.' Felicity glanced at her watch.
'Now, we really must . . . Miranda, shall we get down to
it, dear?'

With which request, which was really a command,
they mounted the stairs, leaving an apparently
somnolent male stretched full-length in his low chair.
But Miranda, glancing back, caught a derisive gleam
from under the long, half-lowered lashes.

Felicity saw them off next morning, plainly trying not to
look as anxious as she felt. As they walked, Wade
supported himself none too easily with his stick.

His teeth were gritted with the effort of moving one
leg past the other, but it was not until Felicity had
disappeared from view that Miranda took Wade's arm
and gave him her support. He muttered his gratitude
and walked determinedly on, displaying the same kind
of courage, Miranda noted with immense admiration,
as he displayed while working in the midst of battle.

They passed chalets, roofs wide-spanned to support
the formidable weight of the winter snowfalls, covered

with slates like horizontally sliced rock. Strolling beside a rushing, noisy river, they saw in the distance cable-cars moving overhead, throwing their silent shadows down to the ground. Over everything the Matterhorn brooded, white with fresh snow which had fallen at those great heights during the night.

'How are we doing?' Wade consulted his watch. 'Enough, I think, for today.'

He turned, and by his slowness Miranda guessed he was in some pain. They were within sight of the chalet now, passing a restaurant. Glass doors swung, catching the sun's light. A woman emerged from the building, making her way through covered tables on the terrace.

Her yellow jumpsuit fitted her loosely, yet it could not disguise her intrinsic glamour, her slinky shape, the consciously fluid movements of her body. As she put down the tray she was carrying, her eyes panned around as if checking to see who was watching her, picking out Wade and zooming in on him.

Her mouth opened on a gasp. 'Hey, Wade? Wade Bedford? Is it really you? Are you staying over, like me? Why, honey, what's happened to you?'

Her white-sandalled feet tripped lightly down the steps. She looked genuinely concerned, pushing at the artificially blonde hair that touched her shoulders.

The arm from which Miranda detached herself was claimed at once by the other woman. 'Come, Wade,' she coaxed, 'have coffee with me. Who——?'

Her blue gaze rested doubtfully on Miranda, then jerked sideways, telling her without words, Go away, will you? 'Can you manage the stairs, honey? I could kill whoever did this to you!'

'I can cope with the stairs, thanks,' Wade replied, counting the steps that led to the terrace. 'But I'll need expert assistance.' With deliberation he removed the woman's arm and crooked his own towards Miranda, who had no alternative but to give him the support for which he asked.

Seated, he relaxed, leaning back, taking stock of the situation. At length his eyes swung to rest on his friend. Easing out his wounded leg, he commented, 'You're as beautiful as ever, Estée.'

'Why, thanks a lot. You too, honey.' She smiled in a special way. 'Wherever else you've been hurt, your looks haven't suffered. You're still one big handsome hunk!'

Wade did not glow as Estée had at his comment. Instead, the cynicism that was almost always present in his eyes seemed to deepen at her praise. His sideways glance flicked to Miranda's profile, then he moved a coaster, studying it as though it were a face. 'It's beauty like yours that a man misses when he's in the midst of carnage.'

He had not looked at Estée as he had spoken, but, Miranda noted, nor had he looked at her. Estée apparently had had no doubts about the woman who possessed the 'beauty' he had referred to.

'So you carry my image around with you, do you, darling,' she purred, 'when things are at their worst?' She patted the back of his hand with her long, scarlet-tipped fingers. 'Darling, are you still keeping yourself for me?'

Her flashing smile passed over Miranda and back to Wade. Then the blue eyes were jerked back to rest on Miranda's hand. The 'engagement' ring shone in the sunlight.

Estée's hand gripped Wade's. 'Honey? Your—er—friend here? She's your—nurse?'

Wade's eyes flashed with a wicked amusement, but he said nothing to put Estée's mind at rest. Should she, Miranda wondered, go along with Wade's tormenting of Estée, or tell the truth? A feeling overcame her of wanting to match his play-acting, and by some possessive gesture confirm to the other woman that

Wade Bedford was as much hers as, by his silence, he was implying.

The waitress appeared, pad in hand, asking in Swiss-German what they would like. Estée, whose coffee must have been rapidly cooling, turned to her companions. 'Coffee, Wade? Black, like you used to prefer? No? White?' A frown puckered her attractive features as they contemplated Miranda. 'Your tastes have been watered down. Who's responsible for that change—your fiancée?'

When would Wade tell his friend the truth about them? Miranda wondered.

'You, Miss——?'

'Palmer, Miranda Palmer,' Miranda supplied.

'What's your choice—coffee, diluted, like your fiancé's?' Her tone of voice was indifferent.

'Or hot chocolate?' the waitress asked in reasonable English.

Miranda nodded, liking the idea. As the waitress left, Miranda came to a decision. If Wade refused to enlighten Estée, then she would, right now.

'I think it's only fair to tell you, Miss——?' Miranda's brows shot up as superciliously as Estée's had done.

'Adams, Estée Adams,' the other woman supplied hastily, eager to hear what she had to say.

Wade's arm lifted and rested on Miranda's shoulder. 'Don't spoil our secret, darling.'

Miranda's heart spun at the endearment, false though it was, but she shook her head. 'I'm not engaged to Wade, Miss Adams. My fiancé's name is Thomas.'

'Congratulations,' said Estée, her tone bored, although her eyes reflected her relief. She lifted her cup high, as if drinking Miranda's health, then tipped back her head, draining the liquid.

Wade did not speak, staring instead at the snow-capped mountains as if he were wandering in their massive silence.

The coffee's aroma preceded it across the terrace, and a mug filled with hot milk was set in front of Miranda. Wade leaned across, showing her how to make the chocolate by tearing open the packet and sprinkling the contents into the milk, then stirring it.

It tasted delicious, and Miranda was content to let the others talk while she enjoyed the flavour, living Wade's agony with him as he told Estée about his bad luck in getting in the way of flying bullets.

Wade's chalet was within sight of the restaurant and Estée walked with them, lingering as if hoping for an invitation. As they paused outside, she glowed up at him.

'How long, honey,' she asked, 'will your convalescence last?' Concern put an appealing frown into an otherwise smooth brow.

Wade lifted a non-committal shoulder. 'When the medics say I'm fit enough to stand the hazards of the job again, I'll return to work.'

Miranda's heart sank. 'When it nearly killed you?' she could not stop herself asking.

Estée's tinkling laugh rang out. 'Anyone would think you really were her fiancé!'

The thought of being Wade Bedford's wife-to-be was so impossibly sweet, Miranda turned on her. 'It's common sense, pure and simple, Miss Adams,' she retorted. 'If it's happened once, it could happen again. Next time the consequences could be fatal.'

Anger, at the woman who had caused it, and against herself for losing her cool, took her part way up the incline to the chalet, and she halted only seconds before Wade's shout reached her. Remorse had her running back to his side. It was not his fault that his lady friend's words had stirred something in herself so deeply hidden that she had not even realised it existed.

'Wade, I'm so sorry.' Both her arms linked

themselves round his uninjured one and she looked up into his face, unable at that moment to keep her admiration out of her eyes—for his courage and bravery, his readiness to return, despite knowing the danger involved. And for much, much more, but only she must ever know that.

'Wade, darling,' Estée drawled insinuatingly, 'it looks like you've got yourself another adoring fan.'

Wade's laughter held mockery as he sought Miranda's eyes. 'Don't mistake her attention for adoration, Estée. She's my aunt's personal assistant. This,' he referred to her arms which still held his, 'I'm sure she regards as part of her job. Isn't that so?'

Miranda, refusing to answer, retained her hold and, as Wade waved Estée on her way, helped him up the steps.

Meeting them at the door, Felicity asked, 'How did it go?'

'Bloody terrible!' Wade exclaimed, sinking carefully into a chair.

'In the circumstances,' Miranda amended, 'quite well.'

Felicity laughed. 'Now, which one of you do I believe?'

'Me,' said Miranda. 'I'm the impartial observer.'

Wade lifted his head a fraction and gave her a quizzical look. The walk seemed temporarily to have exhausted him. Miranda hoped it wouldn't be long before he regained his normal strength, for her sake as well as his. In his present state, he touched her heart unbearably, making her want to run to him and offer physical comfort.

'So Estée's back on the scene,' Felicity remarked interestedly. 'Has she finished the television play she's working on?'

'It seems so. Wants me to look it over, get my opinion. She's here for a break, she says.'

He stretched with animal-like pleasure and his lazy eyes fell on Miranda, a male message written large across them. If that was how the mere mention of Estée affected him, Miranda reasoned, then the woman must be placed high, if not at the top, of his list of women. So let that be a lesson to you, she told herself. Count yourself absolutely out, from this moment on. But when, she agonised, had any woman's heart, let alone her own, ever listened to her reason?

'If Estée's in circulation again,' Felicity reflected, 'then *she* can accompany you on your walks. I need my secretary's services too much to be able to spare her even for an hour a day. Sorry, Wade dear.'

Miranda heard the finality in her employer's tone and her heart took a dive. Oh, dear, she thought, did that mean no more walks with Wade?

He lifted a casual shoulder. 'No doubt Estée will oblige.'

Felicity kept Miranda working that day until darkness fell and the great shape of the Matterhorn faded into a star-studded sky.

'I've been so inspired today,' she confessed, 'that I just had to keep on and on while the ideas flowed.'

Dorothea, the housekeeper, had brought their food up to them, announcing, as she set the evening meal on the trolley table, that Mr Bedford had been called for and taken across to the chalet where a young lady friend had, she was informed, rented a holiday apartment.

Miranda had heard the news with a sinking heart. It was not difficult to guess who the 'young lady friend' was. Estée had not wasted any time in staking—or was it re-staking?—her claim to Wade. And, judging by his demeanour earlier that day when Estée's name had been mentioned, Wade would be a willing victim.

It was nearly ten o'clock before Felicity's flow of words ran dry. 'Do I work you too hard?' she asked as they tidied up.

Miranda shook her head, mainly because she had no alternative. But, tired though she was, she truly did not mind.

'You're young and full of energy,' Felicity went on, 'which means, I hope, that you can take it.'

Miranda walked slowly to her room, sinking to the bed. Rising again, she stretched, trying to ease away her stiffness.

Even as the idea came to her, her fatigue seemed to lessen just a little. She might not be able to go jogging as some people did—at least, not at that time of night—but there was an alternative.

As if time itself was snapping at her heels, she unfastened her skirt and stepped out of it, pulling on a pair of white shorts which she had as an afterthought brought with her. Removing her blouse, she tugged a white T-shirt over her ruffled hair, leaving it loose. Then she sped down the stairs without even pausing to wonder where her new-found energy had come from.

It didn't last. She flung open the door of the exercise-room which she had discovered as she had explored one morning early in her stay. The mere sight of the rowing-machine and bicycle standing there sending out challenges to whoever might dare to pit their paltry human strength against their mechanical workings was so daunting that she almost backed out.

Bracing her slender frame, she accepted the challenge, approaching the exercise bicycle and putting herself into the saddle. It was not as bad as she had imagined. She actually enjoyed the sensation of cycling at her own pace without actually getting anywhere. Slipping from the saddle, she climbed into the rowing-machine and operated the 'oars', finding the rhythmic arm movements soothing.

Fatigue, returning, hit her suddenly. The regular movements had put her into a state of near-hypnosis, exhaustion acting like a drug. She had carried on far too long. Her shoulders protested first, stilling her arms. Her head dropped forward, her forehead finding her knees with a bump.

It was only when a hand fastened on her shoulder, easing her head backwards, that she realised she had drifted into a kind of trance.

'For pity's sake,' Wade breathed, 'what in heaven's name do you think you're doing?' Her eyes locked on to his, trying to draw some of their burning vitality into herself, but a shiver shook her instead at their anger.

He put aside his stick and, with his good arm, lifted her, tugging her out of the rowing-machine and against his hard-boned body. Allowing her a few seconds' rest, he held her away.

'Are you ill?' There was such concern in his voice, her legs almost turned to straw.

Trying desperately to lift her eyelids, she shook her head. It was as if she were drunk, yet it was his breath that held the scent of alcohol. Of course, he had spent the evening with Estée.

'Not ill,' she answered, her words slurring, 'just tired.'

'*Tired?* So you came here, to the exercise-room?'

'I thought it would wake me up so that I could go to sleep.' A choked, self-mocking laugh was cut off in her throat, then a sigh came from the bottom of her heart. 'Oh, Wade, I I——' Some automatic censor control came into operation, blotting out the word. 'I *like* you very much . . .' Then she collapsed in a heap at his feet.

She stirred to find that his hands were under her armpits, lifting her while she hung, rag doll-like, with exhaustion. He gave her a small shake.

'Walk,' he dictated as if he were giving orders to a speech-responsive robot, 'one foot after the other. Come on, Miranda,' he urged gently, 'I can't carry you when I can scarcely carry myself. So walk, honey, *walk!'*

His softly spoken words must have mesmerised her, since she found herself doing as he had commanded. She climbed the stairs, steep as a mountain. It must have been her own room he had led her to, because she knew automatically where the bed was. It came up to meet her, but the pillow wasn't there.

'Wrong end,' she heard him mutter, his strong hands compelling her reluctant body round while cursing his own injured state. 'Come on, baby . . .' In the haze in which she was moving, the softened tone stroked her ears. 'I'm not letting you sleep fully clothed. Out of those things!'

He urged her to her feet and she stood limply, feeling her garments being peeled away one after another, and heaven knew, she was not wearing many. She made a valiant but completely useless attempt to stop the hands that were committing the trespass.

The air was cool around her, causing her skin to prickle. It awakened her sufficiently to make her look down at herself. Something was badly wrong, she surmised hazily; there wasn't a stitch of clothing on her.

There was a jolt around her heart and she looked into brilliant eyes, male, and unmistakably filled with desire.

'Wade, no,' she whispered. 'Don't touch me. *Please . . .'*

Those eyes grew hooded and unreadable, but the desire did not recede. He handed her the deep blue nightgown which lay on the pillow, helping her as she struggled with it. Then he urged her down to the bed, hands around her waist.

'Do you think I would?' he said huskily. 'When I make love to a woman, I like her to be fully awake and willing, giving as well as taking.'

Why was he talking like that? she wondered. She wanted those hands all over her, didn't she, bringing her back to life, re-energising her, electrifying her? But, her conscience reminded her, she was, in his eyes, an engaged woman.

Her hands lifted to cover her face. She was at war inside herself and she was in danger of getting as badly injured as Wade had been in the battle he'd been mixed up in.

She wanted to cry, finding no way out of the dilemma. Why had she ever started this colossal pretence of being another man's woman?

Even though Wade pulled the cover over her, she couldn't let herself escape into sleep. Inside, she was wound up like a coiled spring. She wanted to be stroked, she *needed* to be stroked.

Had he read her mind? He was caressing her now, and her pulses leapt at his touch. His palms moved over her, stroking her hair as if she were a fretful two-year-old, then her throat, her shoulders, her arms. 'I can't relax, Wade,' she whispered, her eyes enormous. 'I can't let go.'

'What is it this baby wants, hm?' he asked, his smile taut. 'A goodnight kiss?'

He was looking at her with an expression she had never seen before. There was a faint moisture on his upper lip, a nerve jumped in his cheek. He seemed to be under a great strain, and Miranda knew instinctively that she had, at that moment, the power to ease that strain. *But circumstances dictated that she must on no account allow the situation to progress any further.*

She turned her face away, but hard fingers compelled it back. There was a mouth on hers, firm, demanding, his own special scent, to which she was becoming alarmingly attuned, tantalising her nostrils. Then she was deep into her dream and, she sensed, alone again.

To Miranda's fatigue-bruised eyes next morning, Wade looked devastatingly handsome, like a bright light that dazzled unbearably. No wonder he had fan clubs the world over, no wonder women clamoured for his photograph and looked at him covetously whenever he went among them!

His brown jersey-knit shirt pulled tautly to the broad lines of his chest, disappearing into his dark, belted trousers. Once again he seemed freshly clean, his hair springing with health, his jaw newly shaven.

He was seated in his usual chair at the breakfast-table, injured leg extended, wounded left arm held at an awkward angle. He lowered the magazine he was scanning and returned Miranda's look uninhibitedly.

There was, she perceived, a recall in his eyes that made the heat rise in her body. She was certain he was remembering what had happened between them last night. Well, she couldn't forget it either, never would, probably.

His attention returned to his reading matter, but she had something to say.

'Wade?' Did her voice have to sound so uncertain? 'Would you *please* not say anything to your aunt about yesterday evening?'

He looked at her again, and his expression had changed. She found it sceptical and unnerving. 'Don't you mean to your fiancé? Did you really believe I'd tell tales behind your back? That I'd call him at his home and say, "Your wife-to-be has allowed me to see her in the n——"'

'No, no!' Her voice had risen in a shocked denial of his innuendo, mixed with pleading. 'Not that. It was . . . that was nothing, was it? I mean——'

'So you're in the habit of undressing in front of men? Letting them see your naked beauty? But then, you're an artist, are you not? With the artist's conception of what is or is not morally allowable; irresponsibly flouting convention, let alone betraying a partner, legal or otherwise . . .'

Miranda raced round the table, hands raised, wanting

to stop him somehow, anyhow, stemming the flow of his accusing words. He dropped the magazine and gripped her wrists, holding them wide apart, looking her over in a sensual, faintly lecherous way.

She wished her red cotton top did not fit so tightly, and that her thighs clad in her jeans were not so firmly outlined. Then he might not be looking at her in such a way, as if she were offering herself for his inspection and heaven knew what else.

Her cheeks burned under his scrutiny and she tried to pull free, but his grip, despite his injuries, was punishingly tight.

'I—I meant to say, please don't tell your aunt——'

'About finding you exhausted?' Wade released her abruptly, turning away and retrieving his magazine. 'I did have it in mind to point out to her that you're not a robot, that you're——' his eyes raked her again '—flesh and blood.'

'That was very kind of you.' Rubbing her wrists, she walked away. 'But your aunt is very soft-hearted and understanding in many other ways. I don't want to upset her about her method of working. I'm creative myself, and I know by experience how sometimes a person's inventiveness can flow, whereas at other times it kind of dams up.'

He looked at her long and hard, then his shoulders lifted. 'It's your concern entirely, not mine, if you have no objection to finishing up prostrate with fatigue at the end of each working day.'

Felicity's footsteps descended. 'Dear me,' she was saying, 'I'm late this morning.'

'Thank you,' Miranda said softly, and Wade's cool glance flicked over her, returning to the printed page.

Breakfast over, Felicity hustled upstairs, asking Miranda to follow as soon as possible. Wade lifted himself awkwardly, reaching for his stick. It was just out of his easy reach, and Miranda instinctively hurried to hand it to him.

His thanks came in the form of a smile that sent her heart into a spin. Moving across the living area, he paused.

'OK,' he said, 'so work until you drop. But don't, for pity's sake, be so crazy as to utilise the exercise equipment to finish yourself off. I might not be around next time to pick up the pieces.'

Miranda smiled back and shook her head. Watching him limp away, shoulders braced against the pull of his injuries, she knew a moment's intense anguish. One day he would walk out of her life, not limping, but strong and forceful, head high, making for some fortunate woman's arms. Well, she'd known all along, hadn't she, that Wade Bedford could never be for her?

Might as well, she told herself, stretch upwards and try to touch the summit of the Matterhorn as reach out and try to conquer the heart of that particular man.

It was Felicity who grew tired first that day. She yawned widely, running her fingers through her tinted, well-groomed hair, and threw back her head, eyes closed. But only for a moment. Seconds later her smile reappeared, even if it was just a little jaded.

'You're young, Miranda, you can take it,' she commented. 'No one would think we worked so late last night.'

Miranda kept her own smile a secret. If only you knew, she thought, the state in which your nephew found me! And what followed . . .

Felicity looked at her watch. 'An hour or so to our evening meal.' Her eyes swung to the mountains and the green sweeping valleys. 'That's it for today.' She shuffled her notes into a neater pile. 'We'll start all the fresher tomorrow for today's shorter hours.'

Miranda was thankful, and made her way down one flight of stairs to her room. Opening the door, she gasped. Wade was seated in her chair, at her desk, using the typewriter. His injured leg was extended, his injured arm bent at an awkward angle as he beat out a two-fingered tattoo on the keys.

'This is my room!' burst from her. 'What are you doing in here?' Her heart raced at this unexpected sighting of him after a whole day without seeing him. The hours when he was out of her sight were becoming frighteningly empty.

He rotated slowly, his face, which looked a little drawn, pierced by two diamond-hard eyes. His dark, short-sleeved shirt was unbuttoned at the neck, his trousers creased across the hips with his enforced sedentary way of life. His hair looked as if he had raked irritable fingers through it.

Brows descending into an intimidating frown, he asked sharply, 'Whose typewriter is this?'

Miranda's spirits dived. The good relations between them of the evening before had sunk without trace. 'All I did,' she said, 'was ask.' He looked at her steadily. 'I know it's yours, to use whenever you want it. But this room isn't. It's m——' It wasn't hers—the room was his too, as was the chalet itself. 'You could have asked if I objected to your coming in uninvited and using the typewriter.'

'And would you?' he asked softly.

'You've got every right, I suppose, to use your own property.'

'But not another man's.'

'I don't know what you mean,' she retorted. But she did—Thomas's.

His eyes grew hooded, reminiscent. 'I can't forget the sight of you, naked and beautiful,' his gaze moved down her swelling shape, 'standing in front of me. The touch of your skin like silk. Or have you forgotten?'

Miranda could not prevent her head replying for her. It moved slowly from side to side, her eyes taking up the

silent message it was conveying. Then her lips turned
traitor and gave voice to it. 'I never will.' Her eyes
closed. 'It's part of my dreams.' Her lids flew open.
'I'm sorry, forget that. *Please*.' He just had to! It put
her on the same level as all Mrs Faringdon's other
assistants who, she had alleged, had 'fallen at his feet'.
Which was what the mock engagement was all about,
wasn't it?

There was a brilliance in his eyes that dazzled her. His
hand came out, palm upward. 'Come, Miranda.'

'No, no,' she answered hoarsely. Did he know what
he was doing to her? But of course he did! She twisted
the ring on her engagement finger, remembering its
significance. 'Thomas, he——'

Wade's face darkened. 'You prefer Thomas's
lovemaking? He's got around to undressing you like I
did? Lying with you there in your bed—as I haven't.
Yet.'

'I'm——' '*I dislike impostors,*' he'd said. All the
same, she had to have some kind of barrier to keep this
man at a distance, not only for her job's sake, but her
peace of mind too. 'I am engaged to him. I—I I——'
The vital word would not come!

The feeling she had for this man . . . It was
infatuation, wasn't it? she argued silently. It was
worship of the unattainable. Wade was the man on the
television screen all the women raved about, even
Penny. He was handsome and irresistible, full of
courage and bravery, but thinking nothing of it, merely
regarding it as a necessary part of his work.

You could reach out to the fleeting image and touch
him—only to find yourself touching the screen, a
flitting shadow, a tantalising dream. That was why she
felt like this about him, along with all his women fans.
It was hero-worship, pure and simple. It was something
she must never forget—Wade was a dream, every
feminine woman's fantasy.

With some difficulty, he stood up. He must have been in that chair for some time. 'So you love Thomas?'

'I—Wade, I——' It was no use, she could not tell such an outright lie, so she stayed silent, hoping he would not repeat the question.

A hint of pain passed over his features and he gripped the chair. Miranda held back. He didn't need help, hadn't needed it, really, for a day or two.

Leaning across, he removed the paper from the typewriter and folded it, along with other typed sheets, then pushed them into his pocket. The swivel chair began to rotate away from him, his gripping hand going with it. In a moment, Miranda estimated, he would be leaning at an alarming angle, hurting his injured limbs.

Diving for the chair, she steadied it, bringing it forcibly to a stop. He released the chair and grasped her shoulder, then swung her round, pulling her against him and putting his mouth to hers. She tried to break the kiss, angry that he had tricked her, playing on her sympathies to get her where she was.

The more she struggled, the more bruising his hold became, and, to her consternation and bewilderment, the harder he held her, the more his fingers pressed into her soft flesh, the more eagerly she responded to his assault on her senses.

She opened her mouth to gasp, only to discover that she had given his lips greater access to her inner lips' moistness. He was drinking the taste of her, taking the flavour of her into him like a man savouring an exquisite and rare vintage wine.

It was only because she was a novelty, she told herself, as she fought for rationality amid the disorder of her emotions, a new female for him to explore and conquer. His hand had found its way inside her cotton top, pushing it up until contact was made with her breasts, first one, then the other, as they swelled and throbbed at his touch.

Pull away, a voice insisted, that's all you've got to do, then you'll be free of this tormentor, this man who's so experienced he's smashed through your barriers. Not because of any emotional feeling for you, but to indulge his own lust.

He had taken control of her now, draining her of whatever was left of her resistance, making her yield more and more of herself to his domination. The touch of his hand on her breasts, stroking across from one to the other, was intoxicating, producing spasms of purest pleasure all over her, yet putting an ache into her stomach that was not a pain but a driving need.

Her arms wound round his neck, her body pressing against his. Even as the kiss held, he stroked her cheeks with his fingertips, trailing them down to her throat, then fastening round her chin and forcing her away from her mouth.

'Bed, hm?' he murmured huskily.

His words brought her to her senses as surely as a cold shower turned on full blast. 'No!' She tried to break away, but his grip on her chin did not slacken. Her mouth was stinging with his kisses, her flesh throbbing with the desire his seductive caresses had put there.

There was fear in her voice. Had Wade picked it up? And, if so, had that fear angered him, making him even more determined to overcome her opposition? He did not stop her as she stepped away, running distracted fingers through her hair, tugging down her cotton top.

'No?' His eyebrow lifted quizzically, smile mocking, eyes reminiscing as they watched the rise and fall of her swollen breasts.

'No,' she repeated. Her breath grew shallower as she regained control. 'I'm engaged to Thomas, not you. He's the one with the right——' He wasn't! Nevertheless she continued determinedly, 'With the right to touch me.'

'It took you a good few minutes to remember that.

I'd got quite a way under your defences, hadn't I, before your conscience sounded the alarm?' That was something she couldn't deny. 'How far under them does Thomas get?'

'He——' She couldn't tell him the truth! She would lose her job, her income, not to mention her only means of reimbursing her parents for all the financial help they had given her during her studies. 'That's my business,' she added defensively.

Wade gave a smile which told her nothing, and walked towards her. She only just stopped herself from retreating. Slowly, holding her eyes, he pushed her top into the waistband of her jeans, his fingertips scratching the skin of her midriff, making it tingle and bringing all kinds of unaccustomed sensations into play.

The touch of his hands began to rekindle the fires that had begun to die down, so she chose challenge as an antidote. 'Will you please tell me what you were doing in here?'

His mood shifted from sensual to neutral. 'My typewriter, as I said the other day, is the only one in the chalet. It also happens to be in your room. I used it while you were busy elsewhere.'

'Does that mean you'll have to come in here often?' The prospect dismayed her. Every time they were alone together, it was as if some unseen force started pulling her in his direction. Resisting it was becoming more and more difficult.

'As often as my creative urge starts to function. Any objections?'

Yes, yes! she wanted to shout. All she said was, 'Are you writing a book or something?' She had not meant it seriously, but Wade took it that way.

'The idea has occurred to me.' He thrust his hands into his trouser pockets, tautening the fabric across his hips and causing Miranda to tear her eyes away from his almost aggressive masculinity.

Still he watched her, his gaze openly stripping her of clothes. She had to say something, anything to divert his attention. 'Two writers in the house! I don't know if I can stand it.' Her smile made a joke of her words.

He smiled in response and his face was transformed as the weeks of wound-inflicted pain fell away. Her heart did a dance and the room spun crazily.

Then Mrs Faringdon's warning came back to her. 'Women,' she'd said, 'chase my nephew incessantly. Which is why he retreats to his chalet for peace and quiet. I will not have it invaded,' she had continued, 'by a young woman who intends falling at his feet as soon as he sets foot in the place.'

What Mrs Faringdon had not said, and what she might well not have known, was how far her nephew had encouraged those other young women to do just that . . . to fall at his feet . . . so that he could trample on them, smiling callously as he did so . . .

'From now on,' she said, her voice taking on an alarming waver, 'will you please leave me alone?'

He frowned. 'I told you I'll need to come in here——'

'That's not what I mean. I meant—stop making love to me.' The words tumbled without warning from her lips.

'It takes two,' he responded coldly and, turning, left her.

CHAPTER FIVE

DINNER was over and they had moved across to the living area. Wade, long legs extended, occupied his favourite chair. Miranda, on the sofa, listened as her employer, seated beside her, tentatively outlined the plot of her next short story.

Thinking aloud, Felicity called it, asking for criticisms which Miranda never ventured to give. Wade was giving a very good impression of reading a book, although Miranda was sure he was not missing a thing.

Felicity broke off without warning, catching a dreamy expression on her assistant's face. Miranda had been doing her best to persuade herself that it was the beauty of the mountains drenched in the glow from the setting sun that was heightening all her senses, not Wade's presence within arm's reach.

'Thinking about your fiancé,' said Felicity warmly. 'I can see that. Would you like to invite him here, dear?' Her tone was so sympathetic, Miranda could have cried. If only she did not have to mislead and lie to this very understanding lady! 'There's a small room downstairs that I keep locked because it's full of rubbish, but I could ask Dorothea to clear it. Tucked away somewhere there's a folding bed.'

'Oh, but——' Ask Thomas there? Even though, in truth, she felt nothing but friendship towards him? If he came to stay, she knew she would have to pretend to so much more than that in front of her hostess, *let alone her hostess's nephew*.

'It was a remark of Wade's that put the idea into my head,' Felicity confessed. 'He suggested that you must be missing your fiancé badly after such a long parting.'

Miranda's gaze, full of accusation, swung sharply to
Wade, only to waver and fall as it met his sardonic
stare. She did not need three guesses as to why he had
made the suggestion. *He had interpreted her ardent
responses to him as sexual frustration through being
parted from Thomas.*

'I—oh,' she floundered, then remembered her role.
'That would be wonderful. But it's term time at the
college he's attending, and——'

'The long vacation is coming up any moment now,'
Wade interrupted drily.

'Of course!' Miranda hoped she sounded delighted.
'I'll ring him soon—er—in a day or two, if I may?' Mrs
Faringdon nodded. 'And I'll suggest it. I'm sure he'll
jump at the chance. Of—of us seeing each other again,'
she added hurriedly, but knowing that the idea would
appeal to him as a never-to-be-repeated chance of
meeting Wade Bedford.

Next morning Miranda met Wade as he was about to
take a walk, his stick at his side. He returned her look,
brows raised.

The entrance door was open and she peered outside,
expecting to see Estée.

'Is Miss Adams going with you?' she enquired.

'She's let me down twice, so I told her to forget it.'
Wade made a move. 'It's OK, I'm used to my own
company.'

'I've got an hour or so off. Shall I go with you
instead?' Before he could dismiss her offer, she
remarked, 'I'd like to see around the town. I haven't
had much chance, not even to window-shop, with your
aunt working so hard.'

Her bright, hopeful eyes must have touched him,
since he nodded. 'Will you wait until I get a jacket?' He
nodded again.

The streets were being washed as they made their way

towards the shops, Wade's walking-stick still needed for support. Busy 'miniature' cleaning vehicles, brushes swishing, were clearing all traces of rubbish and dust, and Miranda thought what a wonderful idea it was.

The shops were a magnet, and she darted from Wade's side to stare at the goods on display, mesmerised by the bright colours of the woollen jackets and sweaters, the ski-wear on sale even in summer. Wade good-humouredly tolerated the delay as she lingered outside jewellers and souvenir shops, rotating the displays of postcards, headscarves and T-shirts.

Here and there, the sun broke through in the gaps between the tall chalet-style shops, emphasising by its very brilliance the shadows flung by the buildings across the narrow street. The town was growing busier as tourists emerged, eager-eyed, from their hotels, their many different languages criss-crossing from one group to another.

Miranda's gaze fixed on a café terrace flooded with morning sunshine. 'Coffee,' she heard herself murmuring, 'I'd love a cup of coffee.'

'You said that,' Wade commented with a smile, 'as if it were one of your most cherished ambitions.'

Coffee with you seated opposite me, she thought as he motioned her towards a table on the flower-bedecked terrace, is what I'd like most in this world at this particular moment. It's this that I'll treasure and look back on one day when you've gone out of my life.

'Are your injuries any better?' she queried, watching him lower himself into a seat. He nodded noncommittally, as if there were more important matters in life than his wounds of war.

Miranda's bright gaze moved over the busy street. The high, wide-spanning roofs gave a closed-in feeling to the main thoroughfare, as if the place were a secret sanctuary from the white, towering mountain ranges looking down on it.

A waiter appeared and their order was taken. When the coffee arrived, together with a selection of small cakes, Miranda offered them to Wade. He accepted one, leaning back as he demolished it between sharp white teeth, gazing narrow-eyed at the tree-covered hills above and beyond Miranda's head.

From under her lashes, Miranda watched him. He wasn't for her, she knew that, but she could look at him, couldn't she? Admire the arch of his brows, the hard ridge of his cheekbones; appreciate the restless intelligence in his eyes, the strong resolve of his mouth line?

Hastily she took a drink. 'Wade,' she said, saying his name sharply to escape the sweet torment of her thoughts.

His eyebrows arched, his jaw muscles tautening in a gritting movement.

'What was it like, being shot at?'

With deceptive indolence he eased his hips down in his seat, rubbing his jaw reflectively. 'The pain took a few minutes to register. I went on talking to the camera, finished my piece. Then it hit me—the agony, the outrage. The attempt to silence the truth which every good journalist seeks to speak.'

An electric car whirred by. There was the clip-clop of horses' hoofs pulling upholstered carriages open to the sky, their passengers staring appreciatively about them.

'Was there anyone around to give you medical attention?'

'I was taken prisoner, found myself in the remains of a house.' He was silent for some minutes.

There were things, Miranda was sure, that he was not telling her. 'A woman dressed my wounds and I was taken somewhere on a stretcher. I must have lost consciousness, because some hours later I woke up in a hospital bed and a Red Cross doctor was examining me.'

He had spoken in an emotionless voice, but his words made Miranda feel icy cold. He had suffered far more than she had realised, and the pain he must have endured became her pain too.

'It's a hazard of the job, Miranda,' he remarked with a quiet smile. 'I came through.'

'But will you, next time? Or,' hope lit her eyes, 'isn't there going to be a "next time"?'

There was a frowning pause and he shifted as if to rise. Then a grin broke through and Miranda felt a flood of relief. She hadn't asked one question too many, after all.

'Secretary interviews journalist—that should make a good headline! Come on, friend. We came out for a walk, remember?' He had evaded the question.

Friend, she recalled later as she and Wade drank their after-lunch coffee on the chalet balcony, Felicity having decided to take a short rest in her room. That was all she could ever be to this man, wasn't it?

'Hey, Wade!'

His head turned slowly towards Estée's voice. She had cupped her hands to make the sound carry, leaning over the balcony rail of her apartment across the way. Her shoulders were bare, her arms, slim like her body, lifted provocatively.

'Come on over, baby,' she invited, moving her hips.

With a lazy smile he raised his arm, indicating its injured state.

'That's never stopped you before,' was her pouting answer, and she disappeared into the room behind her, only to reappear two seconds later. 'I'm working on another script, and I want your opinion.'

'Bring it over—any time.'

Satisfied, Estée waved and vanished.

A few minutes later the nurse arrived, announced by Dorothea. The tall, capable young woman wasted little time on introductions, accepting Wade's offer to move into the living area and getting down to work at once. Having washed her hands, she asked Wade to unfasten his shirt buttons, which he did one-handedly, then helped him to remove the garment.

'I—I'll leave you to it,' said Miranda, gathering the coffee-cups.

'Stay if you like,' Wade answered, his slanted glance both mocking and a challenge, but it was one that Miranda had no wish to take up.

The nurse went on with her work, attending to Wade's arm. 'It's all healing very nicely,' she commented. 'Now I must see your thigh.'

The cups which Miranda held shook dangerously at the prospect of watching Wade remove more of his clothes, and she made it to the door.

Leaving the cups for Dorothea to wash, she reached her room and stared through the window. Her reaction on seeing Wade's bronzed flesh down to his waist had horrified her. Her heartbeats had raced, and she had experienced an almost overwhelming impulse to touch him.

Going to her desk, she pulled out some large sheets of paper and for some time stared at their blankness. Then her hand moved and one after the other sketches emerged, of Wade's experiences as he had recounted them, of happenings he had not mentioned but about which she could only guess.

Half an hour later she pushed her work aside. Resting limply in the chair, she felt exhausted and empty. In expressing on paper her deepest feelings, she had dug unsparingly into her artistic depths. As she glanced over the sketches, it was almost as if they had been drawn by some unknown force inside her, so poignant and so lifelike were they.

Rising, she went to the window again, and as she gazed she saw Wade walking away from the chalet, without his stick for the first time. His step was determined rather than brisk, otherwise he looked almost recovered.

On reaching the path, Miranda noted that he turned left. Quickly she returned to her desk, telling herself that it would be torture indeed to watch him make his way to Estée's apartment, accepting the invitation to 'come on over, baby'.

If she were to be honest, she tried telling herself, she couldn't blame any man for running at the call of Estée Adams' enticing, swaying hips. But why did one of them have to be Wade?

Thomas accepted with alacrity Mrs Faringdon's invitation to stay at the chalet.

'It'll be just great seeing you again!' he had exclaimed into Miranda's ear, almost audibly licking his lips.

Miranda was not taken in by the implication that he was missing her.

'Wade Bedford will be here,' she assured him, and smiled at the sigh of relief that wafted across the miles.

The day before Thomas was due to arrive, Felicity announced that she would be visiting friends in Zürich for a few days.

'They were my neighbours when I lived in France for a while. They're in this country now for a holiday at the chalet they own. I'll leave you with plenty of work, Miranda, to keep you occupied during my absence.'

'I'll be glad to have some work to do,' Miranda assured her.

'Oh, I won't expect you to spend all your time while I'm away glued to your desk, dear,' Felicity declared. 'Not with your fiancé staying with you. You must show him the scenery. You did say, I believe, that he's a student of photography? What a wonderful opportunity,' her sweeping arm indicated the beauty beyond the windows, 'for him to put into practice all that he's learnt.'

Felicity caught an early train, taking a battery-powered taxi to the station. Miranda passed the morning working, putting off the moment when she would have to come face to face with Wade. Lunchtime arrived, and with it the inevitable meeting. But, both to Miranda's relief and, perversely, chagrin, his seat at the dining-table remained empty.

Dorothea came in to clear away the dishes. Sounds of talking and laughter followed her in. 'That is Mr Bedford,' she announced with a smile, 'in a business discussion with Miss Adams. You would not think so, would you? I think,' she went on clearing the table, 'that they might make a happy couple one of these days.'

Heart spiralling downward, Miranda told herself that she would have gone out of Wade Bedford's life, or he hers, long before that event. In fact, the only way she would ever know if Dorothea's prediction had come true was through gossip columns or Press reports.

That evening Miranda met Thomas's train. Wade had passed her as she had started the walk into the town.

'Enjoyed your day?' he asked, eyes on a voyage of discovery over her figure, clothed as it was in a colourful knitted cotton top and white linen trousers.

'Fine,' came her reply, as she kept her crossed fingers behind her. 'I *heard* that you did too.' At her subtle dig, his eyebrows shot up and she could have kicked herself for revealing to his too perceptive gaze the merest hint that she might be jealous.

With the brightest smile she could muster, and a cheery wave of the hand, she went on her way, hoping that the simulated lightness of her step reflected accurately the airborne feet of a girl gloriously in love going to meet her husband-to-be.

Approaching the station, she remembered how, not so very long ago, she had gone there to meet Wade. She had seen him first at a distance and through a haze of admiration and hero-worship.

Knowing him just a little better now, she examined her feelings and discovered to her dismay that they had undergone very little change. Except perhaps, having heard him talk of his experiences, to look up to him all the more. And to fall tempestuously, and disastrously in love—not merely with the screen image, but with the man himself.

As she looked up at the great mountain to which he had lifted his eyes as he had limped to the taxi, Miranda knew beyond doubt that she had as much chance of Wade ever loving her back as she had of scaling that towering pinnacle.

All the way to the chalet, Thomas exclaimed with delight. Everything pleased him: the colours, the buildings, the backdrop of mountains.

'Is this photogenic!' he declared, dipping his head and staring through the taxi's windows. 'I can't believe my luck in being asked here!'

'Hey,' Miranda reminded him, 'officially, you've come to see me. You've got to put on a better act than this of devoted fiancé.'

His eyes swung to her indignantly. 'I kissed you when you met me, didn't I? And that wasn't an act. No one was watching, were they?'

Miranda laughed. There was no doubt that wherever he went Thomas lightened the atmosphere. Engagement or not, it would be great having him there, if only to act as a timely reminder of the barrier that existed, no matter how shadowy and insubstantial, between herself and her employer's nephew.

Thomas had indeed kissed her, and on her lips too. It was sweet and spontaneous, and she had been touched by the gesture. The difficult part was to come. She would have to act as though Thomas meant the world to her, while the man who really did looked on.

'How's Penny?' asked Miranda.

'Fine. She sends her love.' Miranda nodded.

The chalet was empty when she invited Thomas to come in. He stared around, a question in his eyes.

Realising who he was looking for, Miranda said with a smile, 'The great celebrity's not in.'

Thomas looked embarrassed, but replied breezily and, as Miranda knew, quite inaccurately. 'That's OK. I hadn't given him a thought. Great place this—big too. What's the lady's name—Mrs Faringdon?—must be loaded to own it.'

'The chalet belongs to Wade.'

Thomas's eyes grew round. Hugging his photographic equipment to him, he shifted from one foot to the other.

'Sorry, Thomas. You must be tired out.'

'And hungry,' he agreed. 'It's a long journey.' He followed her to the room on the ground floor which Dorothea had cleared for his use.

'This is great,' he pronounced, looking around. He peered through the small window, his eyes as bright as the snow on the mountains, then stroked the camera equipment suspended from his neck. It was, as Miranda knew, his pride and joy. 'My portfolio'll bulge with this lot inside it. That'll make the other guys jealous. On their measly grants they couldn't afford to live in Switzerland in style like this, not even for a day, let alone a week. Or two.' He turned and smiled at Miranda.

'Or two,' she echoed, smiling back. She was glad to have him there for all that he represented, the warm familiarity of old friends, reminding her of her parents and all that she had left behind. Taking her unawares, a wave of homesickness overtook her. It must have registered in her expression, since Thomas took a step towards her.

'Hey, Miranda,' he held her close, her forehead

against his shoulder, 'something wrong?' She shook her head without raising it. How could she tell him, it's not that you mean more than friendship to me, it's just that you've brought back the past, yours and Penny's and mine, growing up together. Suddenly, I feel a stranger in this place . . .

'Glad I'm here?' Thomas asked.

Lifting her head, she nodded, unable to deny it, but not for the reason she suspected he meant. He kissed her, his lips coaxing and young, his eyes hopeful. It brought her to her senses. Had he turned serious about their 'engagement'? Something inside her panicked. Somehow she had to convey to him that it was still a pretence and always would be.

She started to disengage herself, gently but firmly.

'Introduce me,' said a deep male voice from the doorway.

Miranda jumped away, her startled eyes meeting the mockery in Wade's.

'This—this is Thomas,' she said, 'Thomas Mansfield. Thomas, Wade Bedford.'

Wade nodded, strolling in and looking round. 'Hope you'll be comfortable. Anything you need, tell your fiancée,' his gaze rested on her, dark with meaning, 'and she'll supply it.'

Overwhelmed by the appearance of the man who, until now, he had seen only on television, Thomas entirely missed the innuendo.

'Hi,' he said, blushing deeply, staring down at his hand in Wade's firm clasp as bemused as if Wade had stepped out of the screen and into the room. 'I think you do a great job.'

Miranda's heart missed a beat. How would Wade take the compliment? Irritably, regarding it as an invasion of his privacy? She needn't have worried. He smiled.

'Thanks a lot. It makes a change, having my intellect

praised. The women usually go crazy for my—er—physique,' his glance bounced mockingly off Miranda, 'if you get my meaning?'

It was Miranda's turn to blush—in pique and indignation. Was he classing her with all those 'crazy' women? 'Of all the conceited——'

'Hey,' Thomas broke into her choking statement, 'you can't talk to this man like that! He's famous.'

Wade laughed, eyes glinting. 'You'd be surprised, Thomas, just how she does talk to me. When you're married, I'm warning you, she'll need a firm hand.'

Miranda's eyes pleaded with Thomas, don't give our secret away. It seemed he had no intention of doing so. The statement seemed to bolster his ego, fluffing up his feathers and causing him to 'display' like a strutting peacock.

His arm went round her and he tugged her to his side, his glance slanting fondly downwards. 'That's OK, I know how to handle this girl. We've known each other long enough. When we marry, she'll promise to "obey", or I'll put her across my knee!'

Was Thomas play-acting, Miranda wondered worriedly, or was he playing for real? Her instinct was to tear away, but with supreme self-control she forced herself to stay right where she was. Whatever her feelings, she had to play her part too.

Gazing up at him, she indicated his waistline. 'I can hear how hungry you are. I'll get you a meal. Wade, will you join us?'

'Thanks, but no. Dorothea fed me before she left. See you around,' he said casually to Thomas, and limped away.

'What's wrong with his leg?' asked Thomas, puzzled. 'On screen, he doesn't give the impression of being lame.'

Miranda explained about Wade's injuries and how he came to have them.

'Which is why he's here?' Thomas asked, plainly shocked by her news.

'To convalesce, yes. He's been in a lot of pain.'

'I can imagine.'

'But he is improving, slowly.'

Miranda heard laughter, high-pitched and silvery, from the living-room, and her heart sank as she recognised the identity of Wade's visitor.

While Thomas spread out his belongings and found his way to the bathroom, Miranda began preparing his meal. She had managed to avoid the living area and heard the sound of voices receding. A glance through the window revealed that Wade and Estée were leaving the chalet.

They did not go far, climbing the steps to the terrace of the restaurant across the way. The evening was warm, the sunset lingering over the mountains, wrapping around the Matterhorn and turning its whiteness to a pale gold.

Wade pulled out a chair and Estée lowered her scarlet-clad form into it, casting an enticing glance over her shoulder at the man behind her.

An unbearable pain gripped Miranda at the sight of them, but she gritted her teeth and told herself that she had no right whatsoever to be jealous. How many times, she thought angrily, did she have to tell herself Wade's future and hers lay as far apart as the sea from the sky? Estée was a career woman, she wasn't playing for keeps, while commitment was certainly not the name of Wade's game. Which meant—didn't it?—that they were an ideal couple, the word 'permanency' not appearing in the vocabulary of either of them.

'Where's everybody?' Thomas called, and his little-boy-lost voice brought Miranda back to earth.

As Thomas did justice to her cooking, she told him that her employer was away for a few days. 'Which leaves me free to take you around a bit, if you like?'

'Just lead me to it,' he returned robustly, pushing away his empty plate. Rising, he stared out at the lengthening shadows. 'It takes my breath away. If I were a cat I'd be purring!'

Miranda laughed, joining him at the window. 'Shall we go for a walk?'

Thomas turned her in the direction of the door. Fetching a jacket and suggesting that he did too, Miranda led him to the roadway. Involuntarily, her eyes, and Thomas's too, sought the terrace of the restaurant.

Wade and Estée had joined the dancers, their slow, circling movements matching the mood music which drifted on the still air. Estée pressed herself close to Wade—or had he pulled her to him?—and their steps were small, getting nowhere, as if the whole exercise was geared to staying as close as possible to each other.

'Isn't that Wade Bedford?' Thomas asked interestedly. 'I suppose that's the best way to dance if you've got a game leg.'

That, Miranda thought crossly, was putting it politely! In her view, the couple they watched were as near to making love in public as convention allowed.

'Who's the woman?' asked Thomas, turning fully round and staring at the scarlet-clad figure in Wade's arms. 'You've got to admire his taste.'

'Speak for yourself,' Miranda countered with an attempt at lightness. 'She's Estée Adams. They know each other well.'

'You can say that again!' Thomas exclaimed with a broad grin.

Miranda's heart dipped, knowing exactly what he meant. If it was as obvious as that to an unbiased newcomer, then she, Miranda Palmer, should abandon all hope here and now.

Next morning she rose early and tackled some more of Mrs Faringdon's work, having decided to let Thomas sleep off his long journey of the day before. As lunchtime approached, she went downstairs to check on his whereabouts, but there was no sign of either him or of Wade.

Pushing gently at Thomas's door, she put her head in first, followed by the rest of her. He slept on, face down, cheek turned, the bedcover rolled around him. He looked touchingly vulnerable. As she turned to creep out he stirred and opened an eye.

'Hi, angel.' He stretched out a hand. 'Come and kiss your beloved good morning.'

Dismayed, she realised that he was behaving like a truly engaged man. Without an audience too, which was definitely not in the script that *she* was following.

'C'mon,' he coaxed, twisting on to his back. 'It's OK, I'm decent—below the waist.'

He reached out and caught the tips of her fingers, pulling her down on top of him. 'For heaven's sake,' she whispered hoarsely, 'you—I—we're not——'

'This is payment,' he said, pressing his lips to hers in a series of quick kisses, 'for services rendered so far. I'm doing you a favour, pal,' he added, letting her go and looking up at her with eyes that were, in her view, just a little too warm for comfort. 'That'll do to be going on with. You know, you've got what it takes.'

Folding her arms, she smiled at the note of surprise and looked down at him in what she hoped was a sisterly fashion. 'Are you intending to stay there all day?'

Thomas shot up, swinging solidly made legs out of bed, rubbing at his hair and looking so like his sister Penny that Miranda smiled. He glanced down at himself, at the brilliantly striped boxer shorts that left all but the essentials of him bare. His chest was broad and smooth and firm, and Miranda told herself he would make some woman very happy one day. But not her. His undoubtedly male build did nothing for Miranda Palmer. He was a good friend, no more, no less, in the true sense of the word.

'What's so funny about me?' he demanded, her smile plainly puzzling him.

'Nothing, nothing. You're just great.'

'In that case,' he caught her arm and pulled her on to the bed beside him, 'you can——' He urged her back, his hands on her shoulders.

'Thomas, for heaven's sake . . .'

'Miranda.'

Never had the three syllables of her name sounded so menacing, the lips that had pronounced them having firmed themselves into a near-straight line. 'Dorothea has served lunch. If your intention was to skip it and stay in bed all day with your fiancé, it would have been polite, not to say considerate, to let her know.'

Miranda had struggled upright, smoothing her hair, cursing her scarlet cheeks. For heaven's sake, she thought, *I'm* fully dressed, even if Thomas is stripped for action!

'I'm sorry about that, Wade. I—Thomas and I—we weren't——'

But Wade had gone.

CHAPTER SIX

THOMAS was skimming that evening through a pile of magazines he had found in a rack. The editorial matter was in German, a language he did not know, but the photographs riveted his attention.

'I suppose it'd be asking too much,' he remarked, lifting his head and addressing Miranda, who was reading, 'to expect that there's a darkroom somewhere in this chalet?'

'It would, but there's almost everything else. A ski-store, an exercise-room . . .'

'Like to see my course portfolio?' Thomas cut in, already on his way to fetch it.

He spread his black and white photographs over the dining-table, work that he had prepared for the examinations he would need to pass before graduating. There were portraits and landscapes, buildings and people in action. Some shots were of sporting events, others interiors of houses and theatres.

'They're fantastic,' Miranda told him. 'You've gone a long way since I left you behind at art college. I'm sure you've got a great future.' Her hand covered his and he blushed at her praise.

'How about you?' he asked. 'You were darned good. You could have achieved great things if you'd waited a bit and got the right job.'

Miranda shook her head, then thought a moment. 'I haven't forgotten everything, Thomas. I've done one or two things since I arrived here.'

'You mean——' his arm waved, 'this place?'

'I'll show you, if you like.'

Spreading her sketches across the table which Thomas

had cleared in her absence, she waited for his reaction.

'Hey,' he let the word out on a long breath, 'these are great! Where——?'

'Wade talked about his experiences, and I put them on paper.'

'Has he seen them?' She shook her head. 'Why not?'

'I'm here as a secretary, that's why. He's a journalist. Career-wise, our two paths will never meet, let alone cross.'

She made to gather them, but Thomas stopped her. 'Let's have another look.'

There was a movement at the door. Miranda's head swung, then her hands moved feverishly to shuffle the sketches together, gathering them to her chest and shielding them from Wade's cynical eyes.

'What are you hiding?' he asked, limping in and sliding a hand into his trouser pocket, his other, injured arm hanging loose. 'Let me guess. You've tried your hand at caricature and you don't want the subject of your efforts—myself—to see them?'

'You think,' Miranda said slowly, 'that I would satirise *you*?' She realised, belatedly, how much her aghast tone might have given away to him—her admiration, for instance, her high regard for all his qualities . . . for him as a man.

If he so much as scented a hint of her feelings, she reminded herself, it would mean the door for her, end of job, end of Wade Bedford in her life. He eyed the bundle Miranda hugged, his hand coming out, sliding down behind it.

Realising how close to her body he intended his hand to go in his determination to see her work; that, despite the presence of her so-called fiancé, he would not even hesitate to allow the backs of his fingers to brush against her breasts, she dropped the pile on to the table.

Sorting through the sheets, he stood back a little, examining them through narrowed eyes. Then he looked at Miranda as she stood, hand to her throat, worried by his enigmatic expression, waiting for his verdict.

'Hey, Wade,' Thomas's voice broke into the taut silence, 'sorry, I mean Mr Bedford——'

'That's OK,' Wade remarked easily, 'dispense with the formality.'

Thomas coloured, plainly flattered at having been invited to be on first-name terms with a television personality. 'Don't you think they're great, Wade, those drawings? That *she's* great?'

'Sure,' drawled Wade, his eyes slewing round to the girl in question, 'she's great.' In more ways than one, his look said. 'These,' the sweep of his arm indicated the drawings, 'what do you intend doing with them?'

'I hadn't thought.' Miranda frowned. 'I don't know. Throw them away, I suppose. They—well, they just came out of the top of my head, if you know what I mean. I was moved—deeply—by what you told me——'

'That much is obvious.' He faced her, his stance favouring his undamaged leg. 'You and I, Miss Palmer, will have to talk. Er——' as an over-polite afterthought, 'fiancé permitting.'

'Talk? What about? You mean I shouldn't have used working hours to indulge my love of drawing? If I told you I did them in my spare time . . .'

'On the defensive she is, and so quickly,' Wade commented softly, his gaze slipping over her, appreciating the shape revealed by her knitted top, the flush suffusing her attractive features. 'I don't care when you did them. It's obvious to me that your talents are totally wasted in this job.'

'Oh, but——' All her dreams came tumbling down, dreams of Wade Bedford maybe, just maybe, one wonderful day, discovering that she meant as much to him as he did to her, that he couldn't live without her . . .

'That's what I told her,' Thomas broke in eagerly.

'She'd have found the right job if only she'd had a bit more patience——'

'Thomas!' Miranda exclaimed hoarsely. Then more quietly, under control now. 'Thomas, you *know* I had to have work quickly, that I needed the money. You *know* that.'

Thomas heard the note of appeal, of warning—*for heaven's sake, be quiet!*

The telephone rang and Miranda asked, 'Shall I?'

Wade shook his head and made his difficult way across to the extension. As he talked softly, she gathered up her drawings and motioned to Thomas to follow her from the room.

'Miranda, wait,' said Wade. 'My aunt. She'd like to speak to you.'

There was a curious note in his voice, and it was with a feeling of foreboding that she took the call.

'My dear,' said Mrs Faringdon, 'how nice to talk to you. And how is your dear fiancé? Settled in well?'

Miranda found herself relaxing, mocking herself for her fears.

'He's fine, Mrs Faringdon. He's enjoying his stay——'

'Excellent,' Felicity broke in uncharacteristically brusquely. 'I have some news, Miranda, and I leave you to judge whether it's good or bad—from your point of view, that is. I've had, most unfortunately, to abandon my plans to return to Zermatt.'

So, Miranda thought, closing her eyes, my sixth sense seems to have been right, after all.

'I have a sister in Scotland—my twin. I love her dearly, and she's——' There was a tearful pause. 'She needs me, dear. I hope—the family hopes she'll pull through. And that is one thing we must never do in life, isn't it—lose hope?'

'I'm very sorry to hear about your sister, Mrs Faringdon. I'll——' Well, nor will I lose hope, Miranda thought. 'I'll stay on here for as long as you wish.'

'If I thought that I might be able to return in the near future, Miranda, your offer would delight me. But you do see, don't you—this might be a long job? I'll pay you everything I owe you, dear, plus a large sum in compensation. We got on so well, didn't we? I hope, Miranda, that you'll find work to suit your abilities. You're wasted as a secretary, dear, good though you were. My nephew will stay on, of course, so please don't think you have to leave the chalet at once. Let your fiancé enjoy a few more days, then perhaps you could both fly back together. I shall, of course, pay the air fares for the two of you. No, no,' as Miranda started to protest. 'I insist. Keep in touch, dear. It's been so nice knowing you.'

'But, Mrs Faringdon,' Miranda exclaimed, 'all your papers . . .'

'Will you gather them all together, parcel them up and leave them for Wade to bring to me? Thank you so much, Miranda, for all the work you've done for me. And so well too. If you ever need a reference . . .'

'That's very good of you, Mrs Faringdon. I hope your sister is better very soon.'

Mrs Faringdon thanked her for her good wishes. 'Put Wade on to me, will you, dear? What? He'll take it in his room?' A pause, then, 'Oh, there you are, Wade.'

Miranda dropped the receiver on to its cradle and stared numbly at the wall. Then she turned to Thomas.

'You and I, Thomas,' she said, 'are on our way out. But we've g-got a few more days.' Her voice had faltered and Thomas came to put his arm round her.

'Marching orders? I gathered the lady's not coming back.'

Miranda nodded, explaining Mrs Faringdon's problems.

'So you'll take her at her word and stay on a bit?'

She shook her head. 'I've got to find a job, and fast.

I'll need to pack my things and get back home, then start looking.'

'Just a few days, pet,' he coaxed, rubbing his cheek against her hair, 'there are places I'd like to go. Up in those mountains I could get some great shots. They'd decorate my portfolio like icing on a cake!'

Miranda sighed. What choice did she have but to give in? 'Well, maybe, but——'

There's something you could do for me, she was about to say, drop this pretence that we're engaged. Then that would leave the door open for Wade and myself . . . But it wouldn't, would it? 'I hate impostors,' he'd said, and there was no doubt in her mind that he'd meant it.

Anyway, what did it matter now whether or not the engagement was real? In a few days, her acquaintance with the great Wade Bedford would come to an end, fading like a beautiful dream . . .

'But what? Five or six days more, Miranda, that's all I ask. OK by you?' He turned to her, his smile sweet and, she was relieved to note, holding no overtones of sensuality at all.

But Wade, passing slowly by, could not see that. He saw only Thomas's back, his arms about Miranda's waist, the two heads near each other. Such closeness, in his mind, could clearly mean only one thing—a loving intimacy between an engaged couple completely wrapped up in each other.

'Wade!' Miranda called, desperately wanting to prove to him that the opposite was the case, although how she would have done so she had no idea.

But he had gone on his limping way.

She saw him next morning leaving the breakfast-table as she made her way to it.

'Wade,' why did her voice have to sound so hesitant? 'I hope you have no objection, but your aunt gave me

permission to stay here for a few more days so that
Thomas could——'

'Why should I object? Small compensation, I'd say,
for being thrown overboard from your job. Feel free,
stay all summer.'

'Thanks a lot.' Her eyes brightened, her heart danced
a few happy steps. Then it tripped over reality and
sobered up. 'But I've got to go back soon. I've just got
to find work—I need the money badly, you see.'

He frowned, looked at her intently, made to speak,
then appeared to change his mind, in the end nodding
and going on his way.

Miranda stared after him. Having put into words her
intention to leave made it all the more real. The prospect
of never seeing him again was already filling her with
despair.

She took Thomas shopping for souvenirs. Later, over
a cold drink at a café, he counted on his fingers. 'Silk
scarf for Mum, leather belt for Dad. Hope that T-shirt
fits Penny. Now,' he drained his glass, lowering it to the
table with a thump, 'what can I buy you?'

'Thanks,' Miranda smiled, 'but save your money.
You've been doing me a favour, after all.' Her fingers
played with the ring on her left hand, twisting and
turning it.

'I never did ask you where you got that ring.'

'I told Mrs Faringdon that as a student you couldn't
afford to give me one, so she loaned me this.'

He moved quickly to still the movement of her
fingers. 'What are you doing?'

It must have been her subconscious mind at work.
She had been tugging at the ring, absentmindedly
attempting to remove it.

'Let's forget it, Thomas—the "engagement", I
mean. There's no need any more for the pretence, is
there? I've lost my job, and that was the only reason for
your posing as my fiancé in the first place.'

He seemed strangely disappointed, his mouth sketching a downward curve. 'Couldn't we let it go on a bit longer? If we ended it now, it'd mean I'd have to pack my bags and quit pronto. It'd also mean I'd been staying here under false pretences. And—well, I'd like to keep on the right side of Wade Bedford. He's a great guy, and . . .'

With a smile, Miranda filled in the words he seemed too embarrassed to say. 'And he's a good contact too?'

'Sure. I've got to think of my career, haven't I?' he added uncomfortably. 'A man like that could do a lot for my future. The people he knows, the kind of world he works in—with a bit of help from him it could all be my scene.'

Miranda gave a deep sigh. It was all a mess, anyway. The next few days were only a reprieve. Sooner rather than later, she would be packing her belongings and flying off into the sunset. Clouds, more likely, she thought despondently, black as night after saying goodbye to Wade.

Thomas patted her hand. 'When we get home, we'll talk, hm? After all, what reason could we give for breaking it off right now?'

His question touched a raw nerve. Wade's words rang like a hollow echo yet again. *I hate impostors.* So, if he knew the truth, he'd hate her! Yes, a few more days wouldn't hurt . . .

Walking back, Miranda patiently endured Thomas's frequent halts.

'You're clicking your camera like there's no tomorrow,' she commented with amusement.

'Tomorrow seems to be OK.' He gave a 'thumbs up' sign, then turned it down, adding mournfully, 'It's the day after and the one after that I can't be sure about, isn't it?'

Even before they entered the chalet, Miranda was aware of an alien presence. Not only could she feel it in her bones, her sense of smell told her she was right. The perfume that lingered was immediately identifiable.

But when they went into the living-room, having left the carrier-bags containing their purchases in the entrance lobby, Estée Adams looked so firmly ensconced, it was Miranda who felt herself to be the intruder.

Worst of all, Wade lounged on the sofa beside his visitor as if he were actually enjoying her company. His maddening half-smile played over Miranda, making her feel, in comparison with Estée's sophisticated glamour, like a waif who had accidentally strayed in from the streets.

As Thomas walked in, camera slung from his neck, a bag of lenses and accessories swinging from his shoulder, Estée's eyes fixed on him. They trailed his solid build, his mop of hair, his attractive, slightly irregular features. He seemed to emerge from her examination with an undoubted plus.

'Introduce me, Wade darling,' she murmured.

Wade, whose expression Miranda found irritatingly enigmatic, invited her to do the honours.

'This is Thomas,' Miranda said. 'Thomas Mansfield. Thomas, this is Miss Adams——'

'Make it Estée,' she invited, flashing her baby-blue eyes at him and swinging her smooth blonde hair free of her cheeks.

'Er—Miss Adams,' Miranda added, looking questioningly at her, 'is, I think, a script-writer?'

'Producer,' Estée corrected.

Thomas, swallowing a gasp, was overwhelmed, no doubt about it, at finding himself in the midst of people who, until now, had existed only in his daydreams, and whose world, Miranda knew, he would one day dearly love to be a part of. 'Theatrical,' he ventured, 'or film?'

'Television,' Estée said. Which information, judging by Thomas's look of utter disbelief—almost certainly,

Miranda thought, at this additional piece of good fortune—seemed to bowl him over completely.

'So-o,' Estée went on, drawing out the word and subjecting Thomas to yet another penetrating scrutiny, 'you're Miss Palmer's fiancé? She's a very lucky lady.' Her voice had taken on a purring quality. 'What's your line, Thomas?'

'Well, I'm——'

'He's a student,' Miranda supplied hurriedly, sensing he was racking his brain for an occupation to enhance himself in Estée's eyes. 'Of photography.'

Looking around for a seat, Miranda sank on to a two-seater sofa, endeavouring to indicate to Thomas that he should join her. But his attention was most definitely elsewhere.

'Well now,' said Estée, smoothing her skirt which stretched teasingly taut just above her knees, her scarlet and white knitted top contrasting brilliantly with her fair skin. 'Some time, Thomas, you and I must talk.'

Thomas did blush then, with both pleasure and delight. Plainly the thought of gaining admittance, even by half a footstep, into Estée's kind of world excited him beyond words. As, apparently, did Estée. He seemed totally unable to tear his eyes from her face.

Estée's mouth curved in a smile even as her eyes excluded Miranda from the scene. She shifted closer to Wade, then patted the empty space she had created on the other side of her. Thomas, still in a dream-state, drifted across. Whereupon Wade eased himself to his feet.

To Miranda's consternation, he took the place which Thomas had omitted to occupy, his thigh making silent and tormenting contact with hers. He moved and she tensed, thinking, What now? Isn't it enough that he's placed himself so near I can feel the warmth of his body drawing the heat from mine?

His arm lifted and rested along the sofa's back,

almost, she thought, with a touch of fear mixed with excitement, as if that arm had every intention of finding its way around her. A few moments later, her inside curled into itself as his fingers lifted a tendril of her hair and started to twist it around them.

She turned her head sharply to glare her displeasure when, half-way round, the quick movement caused a tug at her hair roots that brought tears to her eyes. There was nothing she could do but tolerate those fingers caressing the nape of her neck and endure the electrifying tingle they imparted to her skin.

All the time, Thomas had been totally absorbed with the woman beside him. He had a hectic flush and was more alive than Miranda had ever seen him.

'A friend of mine,' Estée was saying, 'in a neighbouring apartment has made himself a darkroom. He's a keen photographer—strictly amateur, of course——'

'You think he's the kind of fellow,' Thomas asked eagerly, 'who might let me have the use of it while I'm here?'

'I don't think, Thomas, I know. We have this—er——' her eyes slewed to Wade, but did not quite reach him '—understanding. Thomas,' her hand fleetingly touched his knee, 'have you ever used a video camera?'

He shook his head. 'Haven't even been within touching distance.'

'He owns one of those too. I'm sure he'd let you have a go.'

Miranda almost felt the excited leap of Thomas's heart.

Estée consulted the gold watch that hung like a bracelet on her slim wrist.

'I'm sure you've time, Thomas, for a pre-lunch drink.' Rising, she held out a hand, pulling him to stand beside her. He was tall enough to look down on her and

she, beguilingly, up at him. 'Come into my parlour.'
Her laughter was husky and seductive. 'We'll see if we
can contact Jimmy Haverson. Oh,' her eyes and voice
suffered a considerable temperature drop, 'and your
fiancée, of course.'

'Thanks, but no,' Miranda replied in the same cool
tones. 'I have some work of Mrs Faringdon's to finish
before I leave for home.' She was on her feet now, the
skin of her nape still not having settled back to its
normal blandness after Wade's secret, tormenting
assault.

He stood tall and commanding beside her, hands
pocketed, his profile expressing detached interest. He
did not seem unduly disturbed by his lady friend's
invitation to another man.

'See you later, Thomas,' Miranda added. He lifted
his hand in a vague salute, like someone not wanting to
be woken from a wonderful dream.

Watching from her window, Miranda saw Estée and
Thomas leaving the chalet, deep in conversation.
Wade's voice halted them and they waited as he
descended the steps, his leg still seeming to trouble him.

Thomas's camera equipment swung as usual from his
neck, his tripod in its case under his arm. Watching him
fondly—he was to her the brother she had never
had—Miranda smiled. No doubt he had reasoned that
Estée probably had contacts by the dozen who might
take a positive interest in an up-and-coming young
photographer called Thomas Mansfield.

It took Miranda about an hour to finish Mrs
Faringdon's work. As she tidied the desk, a pang of
hunger caught her unawares. Then she remembered that
it was Dorothea's day off. If she was going to satisfy
that hunger, she would have to do something about it.
The others, she assumed, would be making their own
eating arrangements.

Turning to the bag in which she had carried back the souvenirs she had bought for family and friends, she spread the contents out, lifting the cotton T-shirt with the Matterhorn painted in bright colours across it, and trying it against herself.

Putting it down, she gazed despondently at the assortment of gifts. They all added up to one inescapable fact: in a few days, she would be walking out of that chalet and Wade Bedford would become just a beautiful memory.

Dorothea had left the fridge well-stocked, but even as Miranda looked at the freshly cooked dishes her low spirits overcame the hunger pangs, filling the void with a pain which she knew food would not assuage.

She straightened and closed the fridge, resting against it on her elbows, hands to her face. A movement behind her almost made her jump out of her skin.

Whirling round, she saw Wade leaning against the door frame, arms folded, dark red shirt collar unfastened under a black sweater, black trousers to match.

'Worried, are you, that your fiancé's being unfaithful?' His voice held mockery, but his grey eyes were watchful.

'I—I thought you were at Estée's,' was all she could manage in reply, her heartbeats going crazy at the sight of him.

'I was. As you see, I came back. If you are,' he persisted with his question, 'you should have accepted Estée's invitation and gone with them.'

'Why should I be worried?' she replied with a shrug. 'I trust Thomas. I know why he went with her.'

'You do?'

'Wasn't it obvious? For the help she might be able to give him in his career. In his line, as you must know, contacts are all-important.'

Wade's lips compressed. 'It depends,' he said,

moving away from the door, 'on the nature of the contacts.'

She caught his double meaning. 'I told you, I——'

'Trust him,' he cut in. 'Which must mean you trust Estée, too?'

She moistened her lips. 'Why should a woman like Miss Adams, who can surely have any man she wants——' Even you, she almost added, '—be interested in seducing someone as unsophisticated and inexperienced as Thomas?'

'Inexperienced, is he?' He looked her over. 'Do I deduce from that that he disappoints you as a lover?'

'Deduce what you like,' she answered with a toss of her head. His eyes were too darned perceptive. It was almost as if they had the power to penetrate into her very soul. For one shocking moment she thought he had discovered her secret—that Thomas was as free of commitment towards her as she was towards him. She waited tensely for his next question. When it came, it was so mundane she almost laughed with relief.

'Have you cooked yourself a meal?'

'No need.' She flung the fridge door open. 'Fully stocked by Dorothea. I expect you've eaten?'

'At Estée's? You've got to be joking! Estée sits back and waits for her visitors to feed her. She'll fix a chef's apron around your fiancé and lead him to the kitchen. Can he cook?'

Miranda frowned. Could he? She didn't know, but hesitating for only a second she invented, 'When hunger's gnawing at him, he paces around like a starving lion. Then he might seize a saucepan and heat something in it.'

'In that case, you're going to be very busy one day, satisfying that appetite of his.'

She looked at him quickly, sensing another *double entendre*. His eyes smiled but his lips stayed closed on the subject.

He gestured through the door towards the dining area. 'If I were fully mobile, I'd fetch the food, but——' He looked down at his leg, flexed his damaged arm with difficulty.

'Take a seat, Wade. I'll lay the table. Or,' Miranda glanced outside, 'shall we picnic on the balcony?'

Which was where, lunch over, he posed a question that caused her head to swing round and stare at him, dumbfounded.

'Now that my aunt doesn't need you as her secretary any longer, would you consider working for me?'

Miranda did not immediately answer, her lungs temporarily refusing to release the breath they had drawn in. Her imagination hadn't dreamed up the question, had it? Her breathing slowly reverted to normal, but her heartbeats were still leaping hurdles at the prospect of working for this man.

Wade looked at her with carefully expressionless eyes. She had to fight herself to stop her excitement showing. She must prove that she too could be poker-faced when she wanted.

'As your secretary, you mean?' she asked in a tone as businesslike as, in the circumstances, she could make it.

'That. And, maybe, other ways.' This puzzled her, but, before she could ask him what he meant, he said, 'I'm intending to write a book.'

'About your experiences?'

He inclined his head. 'Those drawings of yours. They were good. Could you turn your hand—literally—to book illustration?'

Now she could not stop her eyes shining. *'Book illustration?'* I—I'd have to think about it, but——'

'Those drawings you made based on the things I told you . . . Come on, Miranda, you don't need compliments from me to boost your confidence. You already know how good you are.'

The warm colour washed over her, and she lifted her

hands to her face, hiding it. Delight, pleasure, gratification, fear . . . they were all at war inside her at the chance Wade had given her, the challenge he had thrown down to prove herself artistically.

She felt his cool fingers close round her wrist, easing it from her cheeks.

'What's troubling you?' he asked softly. 'You know you can do it.'

She shook her head, loving the feel of his fingers entwining with hers. 'That's the point—I don't know. You've got such high standards, that much I know from watching you on television. Suppose I failed you, suppose your publishers disliked my work? Wouldn't that spoil the chances of the book being accepted?'

'So conscientious she is! Suppose I turned down your efforts even before it reached that stage?' Fingers to her chin, Wade eased her face round so that she could not avoid his eyes. 'It would save you going through agonies of guilt, wouldn't it, at being responsible for my failure as an author before I'd even begun?'

His eyes were smiling, but in their depths was a light so penetrating, it dazzled and frightened her. He could see so much, this man, his integrity was so great that if he ever discovered for himself that she had tricked him—not to mention his aunt—she trembled inwardly at the fury that would descend on her head. And the terrible rejection she would see in those eyes.

'Or,' he released her chin but retained her hand, 'let's think ourselves into a different scenario—that I give you a free hand,' he inspected the one he held, 'that I say to you, go ahead and draw. Then we discuss each picture objectively, putting our points of view to each other. After which any alterations, if and when necessary, could be made to the illustrations under discussion.'

Miranda needed a minute or two for his words to register. The sun was rising on her career, on the rest of her life, because if she could fulfil his requirements, and even if, afterwards, she never worked for him again, there would always be this link between them; a connection which might, just might, prove a springboard for the occasional meeting . . .

'A—a kind of joint venture, you mean?' she asked breathily.

'A partnership.'

'*A partnership*? Wade Bedford and——'

'Miranda Palmer. Yes. Your name would appear in the book as illustrator.'

'It would?' Astonished at her good luck, at the promise that his proposition held where her future as an artist was concerned, she could hardly speak for happiness.

'I've never done it before, Wade. You're taking an awful risk.'

'A calculated one. And I'll be here to hold your hand.' She glanced at their entwined fingers, felt the warmth of his palm against hers, saw the strong muscles of his uninjured arm, with its layer of dark hair, side by side with her own, and suppressed an excited shiver.

'Wade, I have to ask, although it isn't in my interests to mention it.' His raised eyebrows invited her to go on. 'You could use photographs as illustrations instead.'

'None exist.'

'Stills from the television newsreels?'

'Look,' he said impatiently, 'don't you want the work I'm offering?'

'Very much, but——'

'So. You're doing a very good job of writing yourself out of my particular script.'

Miranda shook her head. 'I just wanted to point out your options where the illustration of your work is concerned.'

'Thanks a lot, lady.' His smile sent tingling spurts all over her. 'But I guess I know my way around the media jungle. And in that, I'm including publishers of books like the one I'm intending to write. Listen.' He shifted a little more towards her, her hand still imprisoned in his. 'Your work, as much as I've seen of it, which admittedly isn't a gallery full, strikes me as being sensitive and compassionate and probingly truthful. Which is what I'm after.'

Near to tears at his words—coming from such a man, they were compliments indeed—Miranda smiled her gratitude.

'With your training,' he went on, 'you must surely realise that the lens of the camera—with apologies to Thomas—sees what's in front of it, whereas the eye of the artist delves below the surface to the unspoken anguish and truth beneath.' He paused to give her time to speak, but at that moment she couldn't get a word out.

'Well, what's your answer?'

He took her incredulous silence for hesitation.

'Financially, you won't lose by it,' he said sharply. 'Your percentage of the royalties will be well worth having. And for the secretarial work you do, I'll pay you—what did my aunt give you? Weekly, monthly?'

'Monthly.' Then she told him the amount.

'I'll double it.' He waited for her gasp to subside. 'I warn you, I'll be working you hard, harder than my aunt did, and I saw how that exhausted you. Can you take it?'

'Once, and once only, you saw me flaked out after a very long day,' she answered indignantly. 'That was the only time it happened. Of *course* I can take it! And the money aspect doesn't worry me either.'

'So what *is* worrying you?'

She laughed, her eyes lighting up. 'Don't you understand? It's just that I still can't take it in. It's a job thousands would fall over each other to get. Especially among your female fans. And yet you offer it to me!'

'From which I suppose I must deduce,' his voice was

dry, his eyes inscrutable, 'that you aren't one of my "female fans"? And that you don't worship at my feet?'

She reminded herself forcibly of the reason those other young women had left Mrs Faringdon's employ so precipitately. Which could only mean that he had asked the question to test her. It also meant that, if she were to give away the slightest hint of her true feelings for him, she would be on a flight home before she could blink.

So, although it was the complete opposite of the truth, she had to answer, 'Of course I don't worship at your feet! And as for that "peculiar effect" you said you had on the opposite sex,' she tugged her hand free, 'as I said the day we met, you don't have that "effect" on me. And don't you remember,' she was standing now, 'I also said that I'd never lose my heart to you? So, on the understanding that our professional association will be on an entirely business footing, yes, thank you, I accept your proposition.'

Hiding her agitation, she looked into his face. It held a grimness that sent shivers along her spine.

'What I mean is,' she pressed on, disregarding her better judgement, 'that although we'll be working together closely, you need not fear that I'll ever throw myself at you. And when the book's finished and the project's behind us, I'll walk away from you and you'll never be troubled by me again.'

'You've made your point,' he clipped.

Heart beating madly, Miranda pushed through the balcony doors leading into the living area.

'Haven't you forgotten something?' Wade's question stopped her in her tracks. Slowly she turned.

He was on his feet now, leaning back against the balcony rails. Her outburst had wiped the warmth from his face. His eyes were as unreadable, his voice as coolly detached, as only he knew how. It was his television image *par excellence*.

'Shouldn't you consult Thomas before giving your final answer?'

'Consult Thomas?' She frowned. 'But wh——?' Thomas was supposed to be her fiancé! In a flash, she switched her puzzlement into cheerful comprehension. 'Of course I'll consult him. But I know his answer already. He wouldn't stand in the way of my career any more than I'd stand in the way of his.'

'So it's still yes?'

Why had his eyes turned so cold? 'It's still yes. If you—if you still want me?'

'Oh, I want you,' he answered, voice dangerously soft. His eyes did a lingering, unmistakably sensual survey of her face and figure. 'I want you, Miranda. Let there be no doubt about that.'

CHAPTER SEVEN

'THOMAS, I must tell you——'

Miranda was at the top of the long flight of stairs as the entrance door burst open. Thomas was there, but he was not alone. Estée had returned, and with them with a man, tall, distinguished looking and bearded.

'Hi, Wade!' the stranger exclaimed. 'Long time, et cetera. Heard you'd been in the wars—literally. Sorry to hear it.'

'Come on in, Jimmy,' Estée invited as if the chalet were her own. 'Thomas, up those stairs and get your portfolio—oh! Miss Palmer.'

'Hey, Miranda.' Thomas had spotted her staring down. His face was flushed, excitement spilled over from his eyes. 'Mr—er—Jimmy's agreed to look at my work. Do you know, he's the——'

'Amateur photographer Estée talked about,' Miranda filled in silently as Thomas hesitated, but he glanced around at the assembled company and appeared to change his mind about finishing the sentence.

Since discretion was not one of Thomas's more obvious characteristics, Miranda was puzzled. He eased past Estée with as much politeness as his haste would allow and made for his ground-floor room.

Not wishing to intrude, Miranda turned away. 'I'll——'

'Come down and meet Estée's neighbour,' Wade invited. The newcomer seemed so pleasant, Miranda gladly obeyed. As she reached the foot of the stairs, Wade said, 'Miranda Palmer . . . Jimmy Haverson.'

The man's handshake was firm, his smile warm. 'Any friend of Wade's . . . No?' Miranda was shaking her

99

head.

'His aunt's personal assistant. At least, I was, until——'

Jimmy Haverson looked concerned. 'Don't tell me she's fired you? I saw the others, I could believe anything of them, but——' he glanced at Wade '—she's different. Can't you see?'

'That's OK, Jimmy,' was Wade's amused reply. 'This lady's publicly declared her aversion to me. She falls, she has asserted with a resolution I wouldn't dream of doubting, at no man's feet, especially mine.'

Jimmy threw back his head in laughter. 'So why——?'

'Mrs Faringdon was called away on family business, Mr Haverson——'

'Make it Jimmy.'

'Jimmy. She was very sorry, she said, but——'

'Here it is.' Thomas arrived back, breathless. He searched for a surface on which to display the contents of his bulging portfolio and made for the living-room, looking round uncertainly.

'What's wrong with the floor?' asked Jimmy, and Thomas made a dive, plainly agreeing with him. The suggestion, Miranda reflected, might be unconventional, but it was practical in the extreme. This was surely one unusual individual, she thought with a smile.

Soon the open space between the dining area and the fireplace, with its potted plants and brass ornaments, was paved with photographs, some in colour but most in the black and white which his art college studies required.

Miranda knelt beside Thomas, having helped him display them. 'I've never known Thomas pass up a chance,' she commented with a smile, 'of acting as his own entrepreneur where his work's concerned.'

Jimmy unfolded his length across the carpet, resting

on his hip and his hand. 'I can't see what's wrong with that. Shows he's got a good business sense. In this world, if you don't speak out good and clear on your own behalf, then you can be darned sure no one else will.'

'See?' said Thomas, his tone one of self-justification. 'Why should I lurk in a corner when I know I've got something up here?' He tapped his head.

Wade, having taken up a position beside Miranda, hands in his pockets, looked from one to the other, but stayed silent. Then he transferred his thoughtful gaze to Thomas's mini-exhibition.

Estée had opted for a more conventional way of seating herself, one more calculated to show off her slim figure. She reclined, with infinite grace, in a low leather-covered chair, crossing her legs so that her well-fitting skirt rode up just sufficiently to reveal their near-perfect shape. Except that no one was looking, their attention being entirely on Thomas's efforts.

'We-ell,' said Jimmy, putting on some spectacles and leaning forward for a closer look, 'what have we here? Is this young man a genius in the making?'

Thomas frowned. 'Heck, don't make fun——'

'I wouldn't dream of it.' Jimmy patted Thomas's shoulder as he crouched over his display like a mother hen over her chicks. 'They're good, Thomas, the whole darned lot of them.'

'You think so?' Thomas breathed, eyes sparkling. 'D'you think I'll make it into the big time?'

Estée, tired of being ignored, rose and went to stand beside Wade. Her hand touching his shoulder caused his head to turn to her, then turn back. Miranda was now separated from Wade, which she assumed to have been Estée's intention, so she had no way of judging whether or not Wade welcomed Estée's gesture of familiarity.

'By the big time,' Jimmy answered, putting away his bifocals, 'I assume you mean the millionaire class? Of course,' rising to his feet, 'I guess you would be thinking about the money aspect, you a——' he glanced from Thomas to Miranda with an understanding smile, 'you being an engaged man. But——'

'No, no!' Thomas exclaimed. 'I'm talking about making it to the top professionally. Money . . .' He shrugged his shoulders.

'Ah, so you're talking about fame, not fortune. That's good, Thomas, at your stage. I admire your spirit, and your priorities. We-ell,' he lifted his considerable length up from his waist, and exercised his arms, 'looking into the future, I'd say you've got plenty of what it takes.'

He looked over the photographs again. 'You've certainly got an original angle on life. Stick to it, boy, and you'll make it up the ladder before you're much older. You realise,' he turned serious, 'the line you've chosen will take you all over the world? Wife, family, they'll come second in your life, if not in your mind?' He turned to Miranda. 'You realise it'll be "hi, Thomas, 'bye Thomas" for most of your marriage?'

Taken aback—she had been rejoicing for Thomas at this unknown man's summing up of his abilities and where they could lead him—Miranda turned a puzzled frown up at Jimmy, then, with a jolt, remembered her role.

Rising, she dusted her hands nervously. 'If Thomas's job takes him away, then——' Her shoulders lifted.

This pretence at an engagement which she had so willingly taken on for Mrs Faringdon's benefit was becoming more of a burden as the days passed. 'Then it takes him away, doesn't it?' she finished. 'It's his life. He must live it to the full.'

She did not dare to meet Wade's eyes, which she sensed were fixed on her. Did they hold censure at her apparently careless attitude towards her so-called loved one, or admiration for holding him to her so loosely?

'My word, Thomas,' Jimmy remarked, 'you've engaged yourself to an understanding lady here! Hasn't she, Wade?'

'A gem of a fiancée,' Wade commented drily.

Now, Miranda thought, was Thomas's chance to deny their intention to marry. He knew he would have her agreement, since it was he who had asked for the pretence to continue for a few more days.

To her dismay, he lifted himself up and came to stand beside her, fitting his arm around her waist. 'A jewel,' he agreed, 'a thousand-carat diamond.' His lips touched her cheek. All of which, Miranda concluded, her heart sinking, meant that he still wanted the charade to continue.

'Ah,' Estée breathed, letting her head droop on to Wade's broad shoulder, 'true love! Isn't it beautiful, Wade?'

'Exquisite,' commented Wade with a wry smile. 'Miranda, you'll want to talk to Thomas, no doubt.' He moved until Estée's head slid ungracefully from its perch.

About his offer to her, Miranda guessed, but Thomas, who did not yet know of it, exclaimed, 'She'll understand about me roaming the world. She's already said so, hasn't she?'

'Estée, my dear,' said Jimmy, stroking his beard and smiling, 'I sense that it's time for us to withdraw tactfully from the scene.'

'Thanks, Estée,' Thomas said. 'Thanks a lot.'

She lifted a dismissive arm. 'Think nothing of it. Any time.'

'Oh, I've——' Thomas looked around anxiously. 'I must have left my bag of accessories in your place.'

'Collect them whenever you like. You'll always be welcome, Thomas.' Her smile told him, and her audience, just how welcome.

'We'll meet again, young man,' Jimmy affirmed.

Wade saw them to the door. Thomas pounced on Miranda's arm, shaking it.

'Know who that man is?' he asked excitedly.

'Yes. Amateur photographer and one of Estée's contacts who might be useful to you.'

'*Useful*? You're kidding! He's James Haverson, chairman of Spartacus International.'

'You mean . . . Newspaper publishers——'

'And books, and magazines. Yeah, not to mention all the other companies they own.'

'But he's so approachable!' Miranda exclaimed.

'You can say that again. I can't believe my luck. Miranda, this could be the turning-point of my life. Hear what he said about my work?' He punched the palm of his hand. 'If only we didn't have to leave so soon!'

'We don't, not yet. I've had some luck too.' She told him about Wade's offer of a job.

He gave a whoop of joy and flung his arms around her. 'That's my girl! Am I glad we got engaged!' We didn't, she wanted to remind him, but knew this was not the right time. 'If we hadn't, I'd never have come here, never met all these people. Just gotta kiss you, love . . .' And he did, boisterously, hugging her until she gasped for breath.

Through her side vision a figure moved. Prising herself from Thomas's embrace, she called, 'Wade, come on in. We're only fooling . . .'

But he had gone.

Next morning, Miranda sat on her bed surveying the box files that stood waiting for Felicity Faringdon's instructions.

Felicity had taken the news of her ex-assistant's new job very well, even if it did mean that Miranda would be working closely with her very dear nephew who, in her opinion, must be protected at all costs from predatory women—especially in the sanctuary of his own chalet . . .

'Delighted,' she exclaimed, plainly trusting Miranda who was, after all, to be married to that nice young man, Thomas, 'that you've been given an outlet for your undoubted talents. And you're going to act as his secretary too? My goodness, Wade's got a bargain package in you, dear. I hope he'll be paying you well, since you'll be doing two jobs for him. And——' she paused, as if a thought had struck her '—your fiancé's there, isn't he, to——'

Act as a barrier between you and Wade, Miranda was sure Felicity was going to say.

'My sister is progressing well, dear, but slowly, which is better than the opposite, don't you think?'

'Your files and papers, Mrs Faringdon——?'

'Stack them in a corner and forget about them for the present. You never know, I may be able to return some time, then, when Wade's book is finished, you could work for me again! Except, of course, that you'll probably have spread your wings, artistically speaking, and flown off to better things. And by then, also, you might be married.'

Marriage, Miranda thought despondently, was something that was definitely not on the agenda of her life; at least, not to Thomas. The problem was how to get him round to her point of view.

She had tried without success, yesterday evening during a walk, to tell him gently that the pretence would have to end.

'Look at it from my angle,' he pleaded. 'It would take away my reason for being here. It would make me look a fool too, and that's the last thing I want to happen where Jimmy's—I mean, Mr Haverson's—concerned. And anyway, being engaged—OK, I'll be honest—even though it's false, it gives me, well, confidence to have you here as my——' he turned to her, putting his arms round her and

kissing her '—wife-to-be, Sounds good, eh, Miranda?'
He smiled down fondly at her.

It was Miranda, now, who panicked. 'Oh, but,
Thomas——'

'And look at it this way,' he argued. 'If you told
Wade that all this time you've been misleading him
about us, and not only him, his aunt too, how d'you
think he'd feel? Tricked, made a fool of, wouldn't he?
He'd show you the door. His pride wouldn't let him do
otherwise, would it?'

So the 'engagement' stood, probably more securely,
Miranda sighed, than it ever had.

She was eager for work, her hands itching to get on
with the job that Wade had offered. Her own portfolio
was still tucked away in a corner. She had brought it
with her, intending to add to its contents, her pictures of
the mountains and the chalets and the pinewoods which
surrounded her hopefully increasing her chances of
getting work on her return home.

There had been no sign of Wade. She and Thomas
had breakfasted together, then he had phoned Estée,
asking if he could go across and collect the
photographic accessories he had left in her apartment
the day before. Any time, she'd told him, and what was
wrong with now?

Going down the long flight of stairs, Miranda went
restlessly into every room, including Thomas's, where
disorder reigned supreme. In the ski-room, skis leant,
neglected, against a wall, while moon-boots were lined
up as if waiting for the season to begin again and for
feet to be pushed into them. In the centre was a wide
table, probably intended for the occasional game of
table-tennis when the weather made outdoor activities
impossible.

The sound of deep breathing made her heart pound.
What if someone had walked in, a stranger, or maybe
an intruder? Fighting her instinct to escape, she strolled

past the exercise-room—and halted in her tracks.

Wade, stripped to the waist, body gleaming in the light of the morning sun, was working the rowing-machine, his arms, even the injured one, its scars standing out lividly, pulling at the stainless steel 'oars'. His white shorts revealed long, muscle-strong legs, wounds healed but the residual scars again distinctly in evidence, paining Miranda even to look at them.

Halting abruptly, he bent forward, head down, breathing heavily.

Miranda raced to his side.

'Wade, what's wrong?' He just went on breathing raggedly. 'Wade,' more insistently, 'are you OK?' She crouched down beside him. 'For heaven's sake, why are you torturing yourself like this?'

His breathing regulated itself enough for him to speak. 'Physio—darned physiotherapy. Nurse's orders.'

Miranda's hand rested on the taut muscle of his arm. 'Surely she didn't tell you to half kill yourself?'

'If you were in my place,' fiercely he drew air into his lungs, 'wouldn't you want to get back to normal as soon as your constitution allowed?' He still did not lift his head.

'Wade,' she urged, 'take a rest.'

Disregarding her plea, he gritted his teeth and pulled on the oars. After a couple of tugs, she saw his pallor and feared he might faint.

'Wade!' With an involuntary cry, she flung her arms around his bare shoulders. He stilled at once, his muscles slackening as he released the oars. Then his head was against her breast and she was kneeling beside him, stroking his hair.

'For heaven's sake,' he growled, and she felt him breathe against her, 'I don't need your pity!'

'Pity?' she cried. 'It's not pity I feel for you.'

'So what's the motive?'

She heard the sharpness and thought, Oh no, how do

I extricate myself from this one?

'For any man,' she whispered hoarsely. 'I'd do it for any man.' Of their own accord, her fingers strayed down his neck to the ridge of his spine, she couldn't stop them, the contact feather-light as it moved up again over his shoulder-blades, which seemed to judder in a spasm that alarmed her and made her press him even closer.

It was a gesture intended to comfort, but he came alive in her arms. His head jerked up, and there was a light in his eyes that frightened yet excited her.

'For any man, eh?' he said thickly. 'For any man you'd do this? Even the hated Wade Bedford?'

'Wade,' she exclaimed, aghast, 'I *don't hate you*!'

Taut-lipped, he answered, 'No? That first sketch you made of me and then crossed through told a different story.'

Before she knew what was happening, she was across him on the rowing-machine, cradled in the valley formed by his legs as, drawn up, they tumbled her against him. There were angles everywhere, pressing into her, but she disregarded them in the pleasure she felt at the closeness of his embrace, the softness of his chest hairs against her cheek, the demands of his arms, the working of his mouth over hers.

'Oh, please,' she breathed. 'No, Wade . . .'

'No, Wade?' he mimicked softly, and proceeded to ignore her plea.

She became shiveringly aware of the movement of his hands against her. She glanced down to find that he had unfastened her blouse buttons and was familiarising himself with the shape and softness of her breasts, a taut smile telling her that he had noticed their burgeoning fullness in response to his touch.

Involuntarily her arms wrapped around him, and as his head descended she submitted to the hard and probing demand of his lips. He was awakening her more than any man had ever done. And she had to face it—it wasn't comfort she had been offering him. It was herself—*and her love*.

'Tell me, lady, what is it you're after?' He lifted his head at last, contemplating her features one by one. 'Wade Bedford, the cult figure, the image on the screen, the hero-figure? *Just like all the other "assistants" that have passed this way?*'

It was like crashing into a brick wall, yet finding yourself still alive, but in agony. Had she given herself away? And was this where he packed her off, back to where she'd come from, like those other over-eager young women?

The consequences of lowering her guard were too catastrophic to contemplate: the destruction of her world as, in the past few weeks, it had begun to build around her . . . and the crash-dive of Thomas's soaring hopes for the future—his future.

Extracting herself from Wade's hold with as much dignity as she could summon, she scrambled to her feet, her fingers trembling as she refastened her buttons.

'If this is the—the end of the road, Wade,' she said shakily, 'please tell me now. I'll pack my things——'

'Pack and leave?' He swung out of the rowing-machine, and Miranda had to tear her eyes away from the power of his physique. 'Oh no, Miranda. You've so much more to offer than those other girls. I need your assistance too much to let you go—yet.'

The afternoon stretched ahead. Wade had left the chalet soon after their stormy encounter. Miranda, resigned, watched him from her window and saw that he made straight for Estée's apartment. So much, she thought, for his arms around me and his lips on mine. It had, for him been a passing amusement. But what else, she demanded of herself, had she expected?

What was it that the lady called Estée possessed, that

drew to her side men of all ages? Even Jimmy's eyes had wandered repeatedly in Estée's direction. All those men were over there now, clustering about her like bees around scented blossoms. So what is it that I've got, Miranda asked, with a touch of self-mockery, that drives them away?

For some time the snow-covered summits captured her eyes, the bright yellow flowers that carpeted the nearby grassy slopes giving golden meaning to their greenness. Hastening at last to her portfolio, she spread it open and seized her pencil and sketchbook. This she rested on her desk, first pushing the typewriter aside.

Flowing from her hand, the mountains' outlines reached up, their rugged slopes dipping into deep valleys dotted with wide-roofed chalets and sprinkled with pinewoods. She appraised her work with a critical eye, then turned the page. From out of nowhere came portraits—of Estée and Thomas and Jimmy.

Miranda herself materialised too, a small figure a little apart, while in the foreground grew a larger shape, a man, dominant and tall, easy in his stance, in his face determination interwoven with courage, a shaft of pain mixed with a strange vulnerability lurking behind the brilliant eyes.

'Alone?' His voice behind her made her drop her pencil, and as she dived for it her left hand tried to cover the sketchbook. Gripping the pencil, she straightened to shield the sketches with her body.

He lounged against the doorframe, arms folded, dark red shirt collar unfastened under a black sweater.

His slightly mocking tone made her want to retaliate.

'With everyone else over there,' her head moved, indicating the chalet apartment block, 'like frantic bees around a two-legged honey pot, what else did you expect me to be?'

'Such acid pouring out from such a sweet interior! Would it be jealousy?'

Her hand went to her hair defensively, pushing at it. 'I'm not that bad myself!'

Wade's laugh rang out. 'You can say that again!' His eyes did their own lightning sketch of her face and figure.

She was glad she had decided to wear the close-fitting designer top she had bought before she had left home; glad, too, that the cream trousers she wore did not hide her shape.

She turned her deliberately uppish profile on him and stared outside. 'I was working,' she said, then wished fervently that she hadn't told him. It was a reflex action, she knew by experience, that when an artist spoke those words, people always wanted to see the results. Which was Wade's reaction too.

He lifted himself from the doorway and strolled across, hands in pockets. His easy stride, his relaxed manner, told the world and especially Miranda Palmer that he was regaining his fitness fast; and that his very normal virility which, as Miranda had already discovered, had not gone very far down the scale anyway, was hitting top form again.

It rayed out from him, curling round her like a tongue of flame. He wasn't near enough for physical contact, yet she felt the touch of him penetrating her clothing, searing her skin and making her tingle through to her inner being.

She spun round but, before she could close the sketchbook, his fingers spread wide, holding the pages open.

'Wherever I go,' she said, as if an explanation were necessary, 'I take my sketchbook with me. It's like a writer catching a thought on paper.' He seemed to comprehend. 'These mountains fascinate me. And buildings, and people. I love drawing them, no matter who, old, young, rich, poor.'

For a long time Wade stared at the portraits she had

drawn, at Thomas and himself, and finally at her own self-portrait. 'You don't do yourself justice.'

'I'm just an onlooker, standing back.'

Eyebrows raised, he stared at her, but when he spoke he had changed the subject.

'I've hammered out some notes, but my handwriting's so indecipherable, and anyway, I've edited it so heavily, I can hardly make sense of it myself.'

'You'd like me to sort it out for you?'

'Having seen this,' he indicated the sketchbook, 'I hardly like to ask. You're an artist, Miranda, not a secretary.'

'I've already said yes to your suggestion, haven't I? Please believe me, it'll be a pleasure to work for you in any way you want. I——' His questioning brows made her pink with embarrassment at having almost overstepped the line again. 'For Wade Bedford, I mean,' she hastened to add, 'the celebrated war correspondent, the famous television personality.'

'Something you'll be able to put on your *curriculum vitae* when you apply for future jobs?'

'That's right,' she agreed enthusiastically.

'Work to keep you occupied in Thomas's long absences after you've married him?'

'After I've——' Every time, it came as a shock to be reminded of her so-called status as an engaged woman.

Was he, perhaps, probing, trying to trip her up and force a confession, having guessed her secret . . . or was he sincere in his questioning? His expression certainly gave nothing away.

'Oh, that's true,' she agreed over-enthusiastically in an effort to parry his suspicions, if indeed he had any.

'Miranda?' Thomas shouted from below. 'Hi, kid, where are you?'

Easing past Wade, she ran to the top of the stairs. 'How are things?' she called, smiling down into

Thomas's beaming face.

'Never been better. I've come for a couple of lenses, my wide-angle and telescopic. Jimmy's taking me walkabout to see the local sights. OK by you?'

'You know the answer to that, Thomas. See you some time.'

'Maybe not till midnight,' he joked, and disappeared.

'Right, let's get going,' said Wade, leading the way into his room. The bed was littered with sheets of paper, the floor around the waste-bin awash with crumpled pages.

Miranda's hand went to her head. 'Your aunt's so neat and tidy,' she remarked. 'Everything has to be in its place——'

'Criticising the *celebrated* and *famous* Wade Bedford, hm?' he mocked from behind her, gripping her shoulders and pulling her against him. Because she wanted to lie back and feel his hands moulding her shape and caressing her, she forced herself to do the opposite, stiffening as though she could not stand his touch.

After a few moments he released her and she turned, searching his face, but it was like staring at his screen image as, expressionlessly, he reported hard-hitting, emotion-stirring facts. Truth delivered with a blank face were the tools of his trade, but, something inside Miranda cried, he had no right to use them on her! She wanted to know what he felt—about her—but knew she never would.

She used her smile to draw one from him, without success. 'Where's the work you want me to do?'

For the rest of that morning, and half-way into the afternoon, Miranda worked on Wade's notes. The story he had to tell enthralled her and, without knowing exactly which passages he wanted her to illustrate, she made sketches whenever an incident made an impact on her feelings.

Once, she could not work out his alterations and he came to stand beside her. His arm rested casually against hers as he made the explanation and she felt his breath on her cheek. He had not moved away and it was as if he were waiting for her to look at him. The magnetic power of his cool grey eyes was almost too much for her to resist, but resist she did and, to her relief, he walked away.

It was mid-afternoon when, staring at the view, he muttered, 'To hell with work! I need some of that mountain air.' He swung round. 'Get your jacket and any warm clothing you can grab. I'm taking you places.'

'But, Wade——' She indicated the typing waiting to be done.

He thrust out his jaw with mock intimidation. 'Who's the boss around here?'

'OK.' She laughed. 'Just as long as you don't mind if I bring my sketchbook.'

'Thomas and his camera, you and your sketch-book . . . it seems the media fringe has invaded my sanctuary in force!' Good humour underlined his words, not the irritability implicit in them. But a warning sounded in her head that he would not allow himself to be pushed too far within the bounds of this safe harbour of his.

They travelled on the rack and pinion railway which took them ten thousand feet up into the mountains. It was snowing when they arrived, and Miranda was glad of the layers of wool she had added on Wade's advice.

Pouncing on a snowdrift, she started fashioning it with her bare hands. Wade stood by as she worked, watching her, watching also as the piece became a running figure. Others stopped as she dried her hands, exclaiming at her expertise.

'A sculptor too?' Wade commented with a smile. 'What kind of genius am I harbouring within my four walls?'

Miranda laughed, but all she said was, 'Sculptress.'

He bowed mockingly, acknowledging her correction.

The view was unforgettable, and she pulled out her sketchbook, finding a perch and capturing the line upon line of mountains, the people, the buildings, even the train that had brought them winding upwards from the valley, and now stood patiently at the station.

Exhilaration made her euphoric, and she laughed again as Wade snapped her with his pocket camera, the thrusting, pinnacled Matterhorn a backdrop to her busy, seated figure. She borrowed the camera and took one of him, demanding a copy when it was developed.

'Will you autograph it, Wade? No, forget that. I've stepped over the line again, haven't I? Into forbidden territory, storming your citadel, like those other girls.'

He eyed her narrowly, then swung his gaze along the summits all around them. His expression was almost bleak, his gaze restless, as if he were searching for something he could not find.

Miranda put away her sketchbook and stood beside him as the snowflakes soft-landed on their faces and their clothes, and joined their fellows on the ice-packed surfaces.

'When you're in places like this,' she asked, breaking the silence, 'do you ever think about your work?'

'I wouldn't be human if I didn't make some comparisons. My job takes me into some extremely unpleasant situations.'

'And does putting it down on paper—well, kind of purge you of them and let you rest?'

He lifted a non-committal shoulder. People moved around them on the snowy plateau on which they stood, some staring in awe at the dazzling magnificence of the mountains, others laughing, throwing snowballs. The brightness of their clothes contrasted brilliantly, Miranda noticed, with the pure white background.

'Will you ever forget,' she probed, 'what happened to you last time?'

His smile eased the harsh recall in his eyes. 'What's this—another in-depth interview?' He grew serious. 'I've already put it out of my mind.' He paused, staring unseeingly at the Matterhorn which seemed just a little nearer, yet just as daunting as from the valley below. 'Like someone falling off a bicycle, or a horse, I've got to get back into the thick of things.'

'You really intend to return?' Miranda's stomach clenched. But of course he does, she thought, he's brilliant at it, it's his work, his life. 'To get your nerve back, you mean? But, Wade, you're much too strong to lose your nerve.'

He took her gloved hand in his. 'You think I'm invincible?'

She nodded vigorously.

'Immortal, even?'

Her brown eyes darkened with pain. 'Don't—don't put it to the test.'

'You mean, don't go back?' She nodded. 'I have to. Not only is it in my contract, it's in my soul.' His arm went round her. 'Why should you worry about what happens to me? If it's my destiny to die neutral but speaking the truth on the field of someone else's battle, yours is to pursue your career—and become Thomas's wife. Isn't it?'

It was a question sincerely asked to which, in the circumstances, there was only one answer. But, instead of putting it into words, she nodded. It seemed just a little less untruthful that way.

'But thanks,' he said softly, 'for being so concerned about me.' He turned her and his smile lit a fire in her heart. She knew he was going to kiss her, and when, seizing her scarf ends, he pulled her towards him, she went willingly, not caring if, at that moment, her feelings showed.

He put his cool lips on hers, and as the kiss deepened the flames from her heart's fire reached out and melted the ice between them. His hand pressed against the back of her head, and she could not have pulled away even if she had wanted to. But why should she? she asked herself hazily. She was in paradise, even if it did have the temperature of a deep-freeze, and she wasn't going to give up her tenure of it any sooner than she needed to.

'If—when you do go back, promise me you'll take care, Wade,' she urged. 'I couldn't bear it if you——' That warning was ringing in her head, louder, this time, but she disregarded its insistence.

'Is this a devoted fan I've got myself, after all?' he taunted softly. 'In spite of all her emphatic statements to the contrary?'

His head came down and she shivered as he began very gently to lick the snowflakes from her cheeks and lips. Then his mouth firmed once more and she was hard against him, her lips parting this time to his kiss, taking the flavour of him into her and storing it in her senses bank to sip and savour when he had finally gone out of her life.

'Oh, Wade, I——' He ended the kiss at last, and she was weak and breathless against him.

'You—what?'

Even beneath the layers she could catch the thump of his heart. It was their height above sea level, she told herself, feeling its curious heaviness acting on her limbs and lungs.

'Wade, I—oh, forgive me, Wade, but——'

His mouth stopped hers and the kiss was drugging and hard, almost cruel in its intensity. When he lifted his head this time, his eyes were sparkling like the sun on the snow wastes around them.

'Hush,' he said. 'You don't know what you're saying. It's the mountains. You're light-headed, you're drunk with them.'

Wildly, she cried, 'It's not altitude sickness, it's——'

No! the warning shrieked, *stay silent. Are you mad?*

He pulled her back to him, laughing now, as though a wonderful thing had happened, like seeing an avalanche coming and swerving away from it just in time. Of course he had escaped a calamity, she thought bitterly, pushing at his chest. He was too intelligent not to have guessed what she had been going to say. And hadn't she, by her timely restraint, freed him of all obligation?

'It's infatuation, Miranda,' he asserted gently. 'Surely you recognise the symptoms? Worship of the unattainable, the man on the television screen. You can reach out to the fleeting image and touch me—only to find yourself touching the screen. I'm that flitting shadow, a tantalising dream, every feminine woman's fantasy. Don't confuse it with any other emotion.'

It was a warning, no doubt about it, and she must take heed of it, or accept the consequences—the packing of bags, the plane carrying her away forever. So she played it his way.

'Hero-worship, you're calling it?' she said, simulating bewilderment.

'Pure and simple.'

'Handsome, irresistible,' she took him up, 'full of courage and bravery, but thinking nothing of it? In fact, simply regarding the dangers you face as a necessary part of your work?'

'Couldn't have put it better myself,' Wade responded with a smile. 'I'm a celebrity—of sorts, or so my fans tell me. I'm "just great", they say——'

'And they're right,' she agreed swiftly, 'you are. On screen, you hit women right here.' She pressed her fingers to her chest and her smile became self-deprecating. 'And I'll be truthful—I'm no exception. Which can only mean I must be a fan, after all, of that macho male image which appears on newsreels. Not you personally, of course!'

Anything, she thought, to absolve him of any feeling of responsibility for her state of mind. If her foolish heart had committed such an unforgivable sin as to fall headlong for this wonderful, heartbreaking hunk of a man, then why should he suffer from guilt? And, if she hadn't managed to stop herself from expressing her love, it would have meant the end of their collaboration before it had even begun.

'It is infatuation, Wade,' she agreed, nodding for even greater emphasis. 'You're right. I'm flattered by your attention, by your asking me to work with you, and being taken around by such a famous creature as Wade Bedford, cult figure and television personality.'

'Message received,' he said drily, 'flashed up as it was in capitals and underlined.'

An incredible warmth softened the hard aloofness of his eyes and Miranda's whole being responded to this man in front of her, this stranger who, for the first time in her acquaintance with him, was revealing that he possessed, after all, a compassionate and deeply human side.

His arm still around her—hers having found a place for itself around him too—they started climbing the slope leading up to the hotel. Their booted feet stepped forward, pace by matched pace, as they made their way among the crowds to the large, grey hotel building perched almost impossibly on the mountain-top.

CHAPTER EIGHT

MIRANDA lay in bed, unable to settle. It was late, almost
midnight, but there was still no sign of Thomas. Earlier,
glancing out, she had seen him on the terrace of the
restaurant across the way, sharing a table with Estée and
Jimmy.

Standing beside them, was a young woman, slender,
blonde hair touching her shoulders, pad in hand. They
were laughing, the girl joining in, her head back to
reveal her graceful white throat. Thomas appeared to be
studying her with rapt attention. He was no doubt
assessing with a professional eye her photogenic
qualities, of which, Miranda could discern even from
that distance, she appeared to have many.

On their return from the mountains, Wade had left
Miranda to her own devices. She guessed he was in his
room, but knew better by now than to disturb him while
he worked.

He had not told her that this was his intention, but he
had been so preoccupied on the train journey down, she
knew instinctively that his mind had been on his book.
Which was why she had stayed silent too, marvelling at
the white wilderness they were leaving behind.

During the evening she had had plenty of Wade's
work to occupy her. When that had run out, rather than
disturb him, she had covered her drawing paper with
rough sketches based on episodes in the story he was
telling. Temporarily running out of ideas, she had put
the drawings aside.

Tossing and turning, she wondered wearily if Wade
was working into the night. And work, she decided,
throwing aside the bedcover, might be the answer to her

own restlessness. She was sorting through the stacks of paper on her desk when a sound from the corridor made her stiffen.

'Thomas?' The door came open and she swung round, a welcoming smile in place.

Stifling a gasp, she saw that it was Wade who had come calling in the dark hours, his jaw already showing signs of night shadow.

His shirt hung loose and partly unbuttoned, affording glimpses of chest hair, while his casual trousers were taut and creased, emphasising his leanness. If, Miranda thought, his female fans could see him now, would their hearts pound as hers was doing?

'Sorry to disappoint,' he commented drily, closing the door, 'but it's not your beloved.' *It is*, she wanted to shout, *you are my beloved!*

'I saw the light under your door,' he went on, 'and guessed you weren't asleep.' He held out a sheaf of notes. 'Any time will do.'

As he moved, Miranda noticed that he took his weight on his uninjured leg and wondered if their outing that afternoon had brought back some of the pain. He looked, she thought, as tired as she felt.

He stared speculatively at her rumpled pillow, then at her attire, and there was a question in his eyes. *Please, no,* she begged silently. At this hour, with all her barriers down, how could she refuse his request, resist his magnetism, his masculine demands?

It seemed she had been on the wrong track. He dropped on to her bed and closed his eyes, fatigue in every muscle and sinew of him. Recognising his desperate need for rest, Miranda turned back to her desk, holding her breath in case she aroused him from his torpor.

His shallow breathing told her that he was not yet asleep.

'Miranda?' The word came softly, compellingly. She

turned to find that he was watching her. Her nightdress was thin and short, the matching négligé she had drawn on also possessing few inhibitions about how much it revealed.

When he patted the side of the bed, her heart leapt and, in a dream state, she became aware that her feet were taking her across to him, while another self seated her where he had indicated.

'Wade,' she whispered, 'I-I'm sorry, but——'

His eyes flashed. There was no need for her to finish the sentence.

His gaze locked on to hers and it was as if they were in the middle of their very own battleground, fighting a deeply personal war. In his eyes were exploding lights, in her ears a thundering of words . . . *Oh, Wade, I love you so much . . . if you want me, I'm yours . . .*

She closed her eyes and when she opened them again, his were hooded, the lights having died clean away. The battle was over, but who was the victor? Would she ever know?

'You can't,' he said slowly, as if having to force his thoughts from a far more engrossing subject, 'continue working in these cramped conditions.' His voice was cool and normal. Had she, in her tiredness and longing, imagined that emotional conflict that had just taken place between them? 'If your artistic temperament can adjust to it,' he went on, 'the ski-room is completely at your disposal. It's roomy and relatively uncluttered.'

'I've seen the table in there,' she took him up, her tone as neutral as his. 'It's so large, I'd be able to spread all my gear over it.' She had the strangest feeling that, although they appeared to be talking calmly on everyday matters, their emotions, honouring the truce, were moving together in a slow, passionate dance.

'It's in my interests too, isn't it?' Wade commented drily, hoisting himself on to his elbow, 'that my illustrator and partner be given surroundings in accordance with her needs and status?'

'I guess so,' she agreed, matching her smile to his and preparing to return to her chair. He captured her wrist, pulling her down.

'Are you,' he asked, placing her hand against his bare chest and holding her still even as her agitation at such an intimacy plainly communicated itself to him, 'worrying about your fiancé? Wondering, perhaps, if he's making it with Estée?'

Was she? She didn't know. Thomas was eager and gentle and sweet, and the thought of his being seduced into worldliness and maturity by Estée, polished and sophisticated as she was, made her infinitely sad.

She sighed. 'Perhaps . . .' This she corrected immediately to 'Yes, of course I am.' She hoped that, in Wade's state of tiredness, her near gaffe had passed him by.

'Would it comfort you to know that I have good reason to believe your fears are unfounded?'

Of course he did, she thought irritably, because he was Estée's man, wasn't he, and what woman in her right mind would cheat on him with another male? She nodded, attempting a smile.

He conducted a relentless survey of everything about her that her nightclothes allowed him to see, pulling her arms wide so that she could not hide her body from him.

'Do you really need me to tell you that you look good enough to eat? Isn't it a reasonable assumption,' his smile was mocking, his eyes sleepy and sensual, 'that Thomas is too sensible, not to say too smitten with you, to risk losing you for a moment's impetuous lowering of his moral guard?'

'Maybe,' she prevaricated deliberately, relieved that Wade did not appear to have discovered the secret she shared with the young man who was posing as her husband-to-be.

Releasing her hands, Wade continued to regard her

closely, and she shifted uncomfortably under his scrutiny.

'You seem unconvinced,' he said at last. 'Shall I show you just how a very feminine woman makes a male, a red-blooded male, feel?'

Before she could answer, he had twisted her round and hauled her on top of him, running his hands over her filmy garments. Stroking upward beneath them, he met her throbbing flesh with his hard palms, bringing a fiery desire to her body and a tormenting longing to her mind.

He rolled her none too gently beneath him, taking charge of her mouth, stifling her pleas to him to stop, his probing kisses metamorphising her moaning cries to primitive pleading sounds which told him beyond doubt that, if the fancy took him, he had it in his power to draw her to the very summit of total submission.

Her arms clung, her mouth throbbed under the pressure and commands of his until, relenting just a little, he allowed her cheek to seek the hardness of his chest while her lungs fought to supply themselves with air again.

His fingers fastened round her chin, forcing her to look at him. 'Now do you realise,' he asked thickly, 'what a woman like you does to a man's reflexes?'

'Yes, yes, but——'

A door banged downstairs and Miranda froze in Wade's arms. It was a way out: away from temptation and out of this man's devastating orbit. For her own sake, her own self-respect and, not least, her standing in his eyes, she had to take it.

'Please let me go.'

He did so without hesitation, arms lifting to fold behind his head, lying there and watching her inscrutably.

Straightening her nightclothes around her faintly shivering body, Miranda seized a towelling robe and tugged it on over them. She did not want Thomas looking at her in anything but a brotherly way.

Going to the door, she pulled it open as if a snarling dog were at her heels. Face flushed, eyes a little wild, she begged, 'Please, please will you go?' Then she made for the stairs, slowing her pace as she descended, taking time to compose herself lest Thomas's suspicions were aroused.

'You were right, Thomas,' she said with a commendable attempt at lightness, 'about not coming back until midnight.'

'Hi.' He flashed her a cursory glance. 'You haven't been waiting up for me, have you?'

'Er—not exactly.' How else, in the circumstances, could she have answered that question? Waiting up, yes; for Thomas, definitely no. 'I couldn't sleep,' she added, 'so I looked through some work.'

Thomas gave a brief nod. He seemed irresolute, as if something was troubling him. 'What's going on, then, between you and Wade Bedford?'

'Wade and me? What do you mean?' Miranda asked, shaken by the question. 'You know the situation, what this is for,' she showed him the ring she wore, 'so how could there possibly be?'

She had spoken too quickly, like someone with something to hide. Well, she had, hadn't she?

'OK,' Thomas patted the air, 'keep calm!' He seemed to be avoiding her eyes. 'It's just that I saw you this afternoon up at the Gornergrat.'

'You were there too? We—I didn't see you.'

'I went with Estée and Jimmy and a couple of their friends. I was panning around with my camera trying to find a new angle on the mountains when who should I see down below——'

'Were you in the restaurant?'

'Outside it. And you and him,' his head nodded towards the next floor, 'were in a soul-shattering clinch.'

'No, we weren't!'

Thomas smiled, his eyes twinkling. 'The viewfinder doesn't lie, love. I had the telescopic lens on. Now,' he teased, 'if I'd been a professional freelance photographer, think of the mileage I'd have got out of that shot—the great Wade B. bear-hugging his latest hanger-on. The cash that would have come rolling in! I'd have been into the big time . . .'

Laughing, he ducked to avoid Miranda's indignant attack.

'All right, so we were being a bit more than friendly,' she returned defensively. 'So what if we were? It was the—the altitude. Those mountains, being surrounded by all those summits—it gives you a fantastic lift, you must have noticed. A straightforward case of euphoria——'

'Uh, I bet that hurt!' He dodged again. 'OK, it was the snowflakes he couldn't resist. He was thirsty, so he lapped them up.'

Miranda had to smile. 'All quite harmless, I assure you. The stuff of romance, not reality.' But was it? she asked herself frankly, having just left the man in question flat out on her bed as if he belonged there . . .

'You didn't take that shot, did you?'

'No, I didn't. I was a fool, wasn't I?'

'You didn't tell the others, did you, about seeing Wade and me——?'

'Being "romantic", as you call it? No. Although I admit I was tempted,' he teased again, 'if only to see Estée's face.'

'Is she—is she your type, Thomas?'

'Estée?' He frowned, looking curiously vulnerable. 'Those cool, sophisticated types aren't usually my scene.'

Miranda nodded, although she was none the wiser about his feelings for Estée because he hadn't really answered the question.

'Hey,' said Thomas, 'have a look at my Swiss picture gallery to date.'

Miranda stifled a yawn as he dug into his accessories bag and spread a series of photographs over his bed.

'*You* took those?' she asked, gazing at them admiringly.

'Who else? Jimmy let me loose in his darkroom to develop them.'

'I didn't know you were into portraits as well as scenery.'

'Part of my college course. Recognise these guys?'

Estée was there, head and shoulders, plainly caught unawares by Thomas's camera lens. There was the surface beauty of her face, of course, but in her unguarded expression Thomas's trained eye had captured and revealed a depth which Miranda had never even suspected that Estée possessed. No wonder Wade was drawn to her so strongly!

In Jimmy's laughing face, Thomas's intuitive eye had perceived and revealed to the world the deep-down toughness which had enabled such a kindly and approachable man to fight his way to the top.

'Who's this?' asked Miranda, staring at the face of a young woman she vaguely recognised.

'That? Oh, just Anita.'

She looked at him sharply. 'Anita? Anita who? Do I know her?'

'Only if you've patronised that restaurant across the road. Anita Macfarland. She's a student of drama, which is how she got to know Estée. She's working as a waitress to earn some cash to help her through her course. Estée got her the job over there. Anything else you'd like to know?'

'Why are you so scratchy suddenly? I was only asking out of interest. It's a good shot. She's got a lot going for her.'

Thomas grinned. 'You can say that again! But she's strictly a career girl, only takes up with blokes who can help her on her way. She told me so.'

Had Thomas asked her, Miranda wondered, or had she volunteered the information? And if so, why?

A yawn caught her again, deep and shuddering, reminding her of bed. With a shock she realised that Wade might have fallen asleep where she had left him. What would she do then?

Thomas was gathering up his photographs. 'Jimmy's away for a couple of days. When he gets back he says he'll teach me how to use his video camera. Miranda,' he caught her round the waist, 'it's great what you've done for me. You know, getting engaged to you——'

'Pretending, Thomas, just pretending.' Carefully she eased out of his hold.

'OK, not for real. I guess it's you who's calling the tune in this situation.'

'You're right. 'Night, Thomas.'

Wade had gone from her room, leaving only the imprint of his body on her bed. It was still warm to her touch, which meant he must have stayed there . . . perhaps waiting for her to return? And when she didn't, had he concluded she had decided to sleep with her 'fiancé'?

Two days later, Miranda ran out of work. She had seen little of Wade and wondered if he was deliberately keeping out of her way.

Thomas also had proved elusive, each day after breakfast weighing down his neck with its usual cases and attachments and clutching his tripod, lifting a casual hand in salute as he disappeared out of the door.

'You know where I'll be,' he had called over his shoulder, 'if you want me for anything.'

Well, now she wanted Wade and wished that, like Thomas, he had told her where to find him.

She went in search of him, wandering over the chalet into every room but one. That last she knew she would have to try before giving up. Outside his bedroom, her hand went to the handle, but failed to turn it. Suppose he wasn't alone? Suppose there was room in this sanctuary of his, if not for her, then for Estée?

Turning sharply, the thought giving her an unbearable pain, she made for her room.

'Miranda!' Her name, which was really a command, halted her. She had no alternative but to open the door. 'Will you stop wandering around like a cat in search of a mouse?'

He was stretched full-length in a low chair, arms loosely by his side. His cheeks looked unshaven, his clothes rumpled.

'Some mouse!' She smiled down at herself ruefully, but there was no answering smile from Wade. His frown and the angry flares in his eyes made her wonder what she had done to deserve his bad mood, but then she realised that she was not to blame.

The waste-bin overflowed, the space around it ankle-deep in crumpled paper.

'Is that where all my work's gone?' she exclaimed incredulously. 'Is there something wrong, Wade? Are your injuries troubling you?'

He moved his head disgruntledly. 'I've known them worse.'

'So what is it? Writer's block?'

He frowned, began to speak, hesitated, then said, 'I'm beginning to question whether I really want to write this book.'

'Please, Wade, don't lose heart now. You've been getting on so well. Is there,' she ventured, already flinching inwardly at the anticipated anger of his response, 'something deep down that won't let you dwell on it; that hurts you too deeply to recall it, bring it to the surface?'

He wasn't angry, but his mouth stretched in a sarcastic smile. 'Playing the psychoanalyst, are we? Turn your delving powers on to your tame fiancé, not me. You try invading my mind, lady, and see where that gets you.'

Miranda recognised it for what it was—a warning signal saying 'keep off, trespassers into my private world will be sent packing, pronto'.

Furious with herself as well as with him and knowing even as she spoke that she was uttering a lie, she hit back, 'What makes you think I'm interested enough in the great Wade Bedford to *want* to penetrate his *sublime* and *noble* thoughts?'

'OK, I know how you look on my occupation, not to mention myself, with something very near to contempt——'

'No, I don't. You've got it wrong. As a journalist, I think you're in a class of your own, you're unique.'

'Such praise!'

'It's true.' She had to put him off the scent. 'That infatuation thing we talked about up there in the mountains—that was really tremendous respect for your intellect, not you as a man.'

'Is that so?' A threat cracked in his voice, sending sparks up and down Miranda's spine.

His eyes narrowed to a sharp gleam and he reached out, grasping her wrist. Then she was falling, sprawling helplessly across him, her back hitting the sharp angles of him. The more she struggled, the tighter his hold became. His hand wrapped around her chin, lifting her face so that she was gazing upside-down into his taut features.

'This,' he pronounced, 'is what I do to my secretaries when they grow recalcitrant. Show them in no uncertain terms that I'm bigger and stronger than they are.'

Miranda panicked. If he kissed her as he seemed to have every intention of doing, she would give herself away, she wouldn't be able to stop herself responding. But in her present position, with his arms across her breasts like tight bands and the feel of his muscled thighs beneath the softness of hers, she was already half-way to throwing her own arms around him and pleading with him never to let her go. But he became still, seeming content to have her fast in his arms, and Miranda breathed just a little more easily.

'Call it writer's block, if you like,' he said at last, 'but the words won't come.'

'For a journalist,' she ventured softly, twisting round a little so that she could look at him, 'I imagine that must be intolerable.'

'Little short of hell. The trail's gone cold, Miranda. Maybe,' his smile made her heart turn over, 'my assistant can warm me up, get that deep-freeze of a brain of mine to work again.'

She stared at the hard angles of his face, saw the courage implicit in his obstinate chin, the determination in his jaw; saw the warmth in his eyes and, deeper still, the detached aloofness that came through on those newsreels he had appeared in.

Never, she advised herself desperately, get emotionally entangled with this man. All right, she loved him, there was no getting away from that, but that was her secret, and surely you could keep a secret all your life if you really tried?

Wade's eyes were very dark now, his mouth close to hers. 'Come on, partner,' he coaxed, 'give me some of the heat from your fire, let me warm myself in its glow. Help me, my Girl Friday,' his hands closed with exquisite possession over her breasts, his lips sprinkling minuscule kisses across hers, 'to thaw out.'

Then he kissed her consumingly, hungrily, swamping her own personality with the force of his, and she willingly drowned in the heat of his desire.

Lifting his head, he smiled mockingly into her

bemused eyes. 'That's better,' he commented, looking lingeringly at each feature, his hands still holding her possessively. 'The wheels of my brain have been de-iced and are starting, very slowly, to grind into action again.' There was a gleam in his eye as he added, 'I'm still cold, though. A bit more of your warmth might speed up the process . . .' His head began to lower again, but Miranda twisted her head away.

'You're blatantly using me!' she accused, trying without success to dislodge his hands from her breasts as they burgeoned tellingly beneath his hold. His eyes hardened, but she had to go on. 'Why don't you go to Estée and use *her* as a means of lubricating your mind's mechanism? She's your woman, after all.'

'Is she?' he muttered, absorbed with tracing a tingling trail with his tongue-tip around Miranda's left ear. 'Estée is varied in her tastes. It's Jimmy when he's there. In his absence, I take his place on her menu.' Which revealed exactly nothing, Miranda thought, about how Wade felt about Estée.

She moaned at the shivers that were coursing through her under the sensual onslaught of his tongue. Then she struggled, desperate to free herself before her lips, out of control, allowed themselves to be pulled back by the powerful magnet in his.

He let her go, and she scrambled to her feet, straightening her clothes. 'It's obvious,' she exclaimed, still throbbing from his devastating arousal technique, 'that you're missing the lady, otherwise you wouldn't have been so desperate as to make do with me. After all,' her eyes blazed, 'her sexuality is so powerful that anything I'm able to offer must be much poorer in quality than hers.'

'My word,' drawled Wade, his eyes wandering over her, undressing her in his mind, Miranda was sure, 'your fiancé's given you one hell of an inferiority complex! You've hinted before at his inexperience, and

I'm beginning to believe it. Any time you need advice, theoretical or practical, I'd be delighted . . . But of course,' he jeered, 'you wouldn't take it from me, a man you only like—if "like" isn't too strong a word—for his intellect, yet heartily despise as an example of the male of the species.'

The telephone rang and, as Miranda hesitated, Wade swung his arm to take the call. 'Hi, Estée.'

It sounded, Miranda thought, as a painful shaft of jealousy shot through her, as if he was delighted to hear from his lady friend. And why shouldn't he be? she reflected sadly, going on her way. What had just happened between herself and Wade had meant absolutely nothing . . . to him.

'This evening?' she heard him add. 'Yes, why not?'

The ski-room as a place to work, Miranda discovered, couldn't be bettered. Not only could she spread herself physically, her artistic imagination seemed to fill out and flower, like leaves and buds in the summer's warmth.

There were a few wooden benches and, in a corner, a boiler, unused at that time of year. Ski equipment lay discarded on the floor, which was covered with a rough matting. None of this, Miranda decided, would disturb her train of thought.

The ski clothes that had hung on pegs she had gathered into one corner, piling them one on the other. She hoped their owners wouldn't mind. When the skiing season started again, Wade's book would have been completed and—she had to face the fact—she herself would be gone, and the clothes could then be returned to their rightful places.

Seating herself at the table, she sorted through her drawings, and selected a few at random. Raking in her holdall, she arranged her pastels in a row and started shading in the pencil drawings she had made. They sprang to life under her moving fingers, her imagination, helped by her memories of the television newsreels in which Wade had appeared, filling in the gaps in her knowledge of the terrain surrounding the area Wade was writing about.

She was so absorbed that she did not hear the footsteps that were approaching until they had reached the doorway, halting there. She had a few precious seconds in which to shuffle together and hide the drawings she was working on.

'Wade,' she exclaimed, leaning on her arms on the covered pictures, 'you gave me such a fright!'

Even before she had turned to greet the newcomer, she had guessed who it was. Only one man could make her skin prickle like that. He stood beside her, hands in pockets, eyes amused.

'You look,' he remarked, 'like a kitten who's been fed a saucer of cream and is now licking its paws.'

Miranda laughed, still leaning forward on her arms. 'It makes a wonderful studio, this room, that's why. It was a brilliant idea of yours that I should use it.'

Wade bowed ironically.

She smiled up at him and his hands came from behind to fasten on her shoulders. She shivered as his fingers exerted pressure on her neck, turning it seductively into a caress.

He glanced down at her arms, still protecting her drawings, and his suspicions were aroused. 'I never met an artist so secretive about her work! What are you hiding now?'

'Nothing . . . just a few doodles.'

'Ah,' his eyelids drooped, his hands moving in a massaging movement over her shoulders, 'doodles—the great psychological giveaway. Earlier, you tried your analytical skills on me. Maybe,' without warning, he grasped her bare upper arms, 'I should return the compliment and psychoanalyse you.'

'No, no,' with her elbow, Miranda slid a folder on top of the pictures, 'when they're finished you can see them. Half-done work shouldn't be shown to anybody, especially the uninitiated.'

'And especially uncultured types like journalists, hm?' Wade commented grimly.

'That's not true.' If she showed them to him before they were finished, and he verbally tore them to shreds, her confidence would desert her entirely.

She stiffened all her muscles against him, scared of his intention because she knew, if he persisted, that she just wouldn't be able to resist him. His jaw came out in response to her challenge to his superior strength. It took him only a couple of seconds to shift her chair and jerk her to her feet.

He prised her arms open and forced them behind her back.

'Let me see them,' he commanded, his eyes caught and held by the provocative thrust of her breasts.

Miranda's heart throbbed with a dangerous excitement. They were engaged in a furious battle, the clash of steel within his eyes striking to her very depths. His male vigour—she could actually feel its vibrations—reached out to the essential femininity within her, but she told herself fiercely that if she responded in the way her body yearned to do, and his masculinity demanded, the barriers between them would go crashing and nothing could hold them apart.

It wasn't a matter of personalities, she argued silently, it wasn't Wade Bedford wanting Miranda Palmer and no other woman, it was his ingrained sensuality demanding satisfaction from *any* woman. That was something she *must* remember.

Slowly, his expression brooding, eyes dark with intent, he impelled her towards him and, imprisoned as she was, there was nothing she could do to hold off his kiss. Nor, at that moment, did she want to.

As he twisted her sideways and closed his mouth over hers, a tiny moan escaped her. His hands found her breasts, moulding and stroking, causing sensation after pleasurable sensation to course through her. Her breathing shallow, she melted against him and, as his leg thrust between hers, her body began to tremble with an almost irresistible desire.

Lifting his head, Wade turned his narrowed eyes upon her, his breath playing over her flushed face.

'Now show them to me,' he gritted, ignoring her attempts to free her wrists from his punishing grip.

'My hands,' she whispered, 'please let them go. If you—if you damage them, I won't be able to draw, and then my life wouldn't be worth living.'

With a strangely twisted smile, he did as she had asked. As the blood supply rushed back, Miranda rubbed urgently at her painful wrists. For a moment he watched, then took her hands one at a time, massaging the life back into them.

'Show me them,' he said softly, holding her eyes. 'Show me your work.' Still she hesitated, loving the movement of his palms over the sensitive skin of her wrists, but fearing that he might detect the hectic beat of her pulse. 'What are you afraid of? Criticism?' He saw from the flicker of her lashes that he was right. 'I promise I won't crush your ego, nor your artistic sensibilities.'

He freed her at last.

'I'm sorry,' she said, lowering herself a little shakily into the chair, 'that I tried to keep them a secret. I'm new to the illustration scene. As the author, you have every right to see them, whatever stage they're at.' She moved to uncover her work. 'If you want to tear them to pieces—literally—go ahead. I can take it.' Could she? she wondered, and steeled herself for his disappointment; worse, his lukewarm praise.

As he sorted through the sheets of cartridge paper,

she closed her eyes. If he didn't like her interpretation of his descriptions, or her style; if her abilities fell below his high standards, this could mean the end—of their collaboration, even their acquaintance. Not since she had awaited the result of her college examinations, the class of her degree—not even knowing whether she had attained a qualification at all—had she felt so tense, nor so apprehensive.

At last Wade spoke. Only minutes had passed, but to Miranda it seemed more like hours.

'Open your eyes.' His fingers lifted her chin, and the warmth in his appraisal set her heart in a spin. 'What can I say to you but—thanks. Your vision and mine—they seem to coincide to a degree I would never have dreamed of. These are excellent—all of them. Just go on like that, and the illustrator of the book will be sought after even more than the author—if *he's* sought after at all!'

'You're exaggerating,' she protested, laughing, 'but thanks for the praise. My own artistic know-how tells me they could be improved. I'm very critical of my own work——'

'And you should be. If you, as the creator, can't see the imperfections, then you're doomed, because you can be darned sure that the art critics, every one of them, will, and tell not only you, but the whole world. And where would Miss Miranda Palmer's career be then?'

'In tatters, probably.' She smiled, relief unclasping her hands, putting lights back into her eyes. This man's approval, let alone praise, had meant the world to her.

'You do realise,' she reminded him, 'that some time we'll have to get together and talk about the printing aspect, like size of drawings, layout and so on?'

'Don't pressure me, lady. That writer's block you helped me overcome, it's got smaller, but it hasn't disappeared altogether.'

'Perhaps you need me to psychoanalyse you, after all?'

Wade made a playful thrust at her chin. 'Tonight Estée's giving a party.'

'I hope you enjoy it,' Miranda responded stiffly.

'I fully intend to. You're invited.'

'Thanks, but I——'

'I've accepted on your behalf. Work can wait,' he clipped. 'You need a break. You're coming.'

'Is that an order?'

'It's an order—from your partner,' his fingers grasped her chin and she found his stare hypnotic, 'who is also your boss. Get it?'

Mesmerised, seeking in the depths of his eyes for a message which she knew in her heart would never be there for her, Miranda could only nod.

Somewhere in the chalet a door slammed. Wade released her at once. Withdrawing abruptly into himself, he went on his way.

Her eyes and her heart followed him, but she called them to heel angrily. A partnership, he had called this collaboration of theirs—strictly business and no nonsense. In the few moments' silence that ensued, she made some attempt to bring order to her thoughts and arrange a smile of greeting.

'Hey!' exclaimed Thomas from the doorway and looking around. 'What are you doing in here?'

'Welcome to my studio,' said Miranda, inviting him to take a seat and proceeding to explain how she came to be there.

Towards the end of the afternoon, a few handwritten sheets appeared on Miranda's desk. Skimming through them, she realised that, although Wade's 'block' had not been completely breached, more than a trickle of ideas had escaped over and around it.

Skimming through the notes, she picked up a new

name—Patti, Patti Burton. Patti, it seemed, was a lady; she was also a journalist, a colleague—a close one—of Wade's. What other part did she play in his life? Was she 'close' too, in other ways?

Pulling out her sketchpad, Miranda moved her hand across the paper, but for once her imagination closed down. The woman called Patti seemed to have had an inhibiting effect on it. With a sigh, Miranda pushed the pad aside. She would type Wade's notes instead and wait for her artistic eye to open again.

Thomas escorted her to Estée's apartment, Wade having gone on in advance.

'A party', Wade had described Estée's social gathering, so how, Miranda wondered, should she dress? But, she told herself, no matter how carefully she might choose her clothes, she would never be able to outshine those of her hostess. So she didn't even try.

Selecting an oyster pink silk shirt that plunged a little if one or two buttons were left unfastened, giving the simple style a party-like air, she added a wrap-around cream linen-type skirt that flattered her hips and enhanced the slimness of her waist.

The chunky white beads, matching earrings and white sandals balanced each other, adding, she hoped, a touch of chic. The entire outfit, if not exactly qualifying for the label 'glamorous', none the less lent to her faintly nervous self a semblance of confidence. Although this, as she knew full well, would be shattered the moment her own choice of party wear came face to face with Estée's—even, she thought ruefully, turning away from the mirror, if that lady were wearing sackcloth and ashes!

Thomas knew his way around. The way he sprinted up the steps and opened the door, quite forgetting to stand back and allow Miranda to precede him, as a thoughtful fiancé should, told her just how at home he felt in Estée Adams' residence.

In the background, the taped sound of yodelling voices rose above the harmonious cadences of a town band. The result, Miranda had to acknowledge as her spirits lifted, was both atmospheric and jolly.

The moment they walked in, Thomas detached himself from her, wandering through opened sliding doors into a dining area. With hungry eyes he scanned tables laden with enticing savouries and sweet confections.

Wade's eyes, having swung at once towards Miranda, held a strange expression, a kind of painter's palette of satire, mockery and, there was no mistaking it, uninhibited sensuality.

He was doing it deliberately, Miranda was sure, to embarrass her. There was laughter, too, in his look. In his dark-blue shirt and fawn belted trousers, his thick hair just a little tousled as if coaxing female fingers had run through it, he looked fit and virile and heartbreaking, and she wanted to run to him and touch him, like any worshipping female fan.

Swiftly, to hide her inner turmoil from his lightning-fast perception, Miranda joined Thomas.

'Smashing grub!' exclaimed Thomas. 'I can't wait!'

'Is this mini-feast your work, Estée?' Miranda asked in astonishment, remembering the woman's reputation as a poor cook.

'It's Dorothea's,' Thomas answered for her. 'And her two daughters'.'

'Thomas,' Jimmy called, 'how about a shot?' He indicated the colourful display. 'You could have a go at sending it to a catering magazine.'

'One of yours?' asked Thomas, immediately readying his photographic gear for action.

Miranda exclaimed at his cool impudence, but Jimmy laughed. 'You never know your luck, son,' was his unperturbed reply.

Thomas lined up his camera with elaborate care, and

there was a series of brilliant flashes as he took the shots.

Dazzled, Miranda turned away, noting as she did so that Wade was as much at home in his lady friend's apartment as she had guessed he might be. So why, she questioned herself severely, was her heart misguided enough to sink at the sight of him reclining cornerwise on a sofa, as if he belonged there? And Estée, beside him, looking as though she, in turn, belonged to him.

Her eyes bouncing off the shining blue satin of Estée's leisure suit, Miranda knew she had been right in not even trying to beat Estée at her own game. The woman's glamour, not to mention the sexuality implicit in every movement she made, was clearly calculated to hit every newcomer, especially the male of the species, between the eyes.

Thomas, in spite of their mock engagement, had been no exception. From the start, he had hardly been able to tear his eyes from the deep cleft, the gold-bedecked throat, the matching bangles drawing attention to the slim wrists.

If it hadn't looked so obvious, Miranda thought, she would have tweaked Thomas's arm to break the spell and remind him of his position as her 'fiancé'.

Jimmy Haverson, smile in place, missing nothing, was there, back from his travels, seated in his favourite place, on the floor, back against the wall, his legs casually outstretched and crossed at the ankles. His manner, like Wade's, was relaxed, and he too looked as if he knew everything there was to know about Estée's place. He raised his glass towards Miranda and Thomas.

'To the happy couple. Welcome, you two. Have a drink.' An eyebrow lifted, laughter in his face. 'Still in love?'

Thomas's head jerked like a puppet's, then he recovered himself. 'Why shouldn't we be?' He sounded curiously on the defensive.

'Yes, very much,' Miranda filled in, surreptitiously crossing her fingers on both hands at the untruth. How else, she wondered worriedly, could she counteract in their listeners' minds Thomas's odd lack of conviction?

She felt Wade's sardonic stare, but kept her head averted.

'Thomas,' Estée's smooth bare arm, a mere whisper from Wade's, waved vaguely towards a collection of bottles, 'help yourself and your fiancée to a drink. You know your way about this place blindfold by now, don't you?'

So, Miranda reflected, she'd been right about Thomas. Here was yet another man so familiar with these surroundings that it was almost as if he lived there! Did Estée have this effect on all the males who came within her mystic circle?

The apartment, or as much as Miranda had seen of it, was furnished with taste and simplicity. The living area where the party was being held was both functional and bright.

As the doorbell chimed, Estée rose gracefully, shedding as she did so both a trace of seductive perfume and an equally seductive smile on to the man beside her. Hips swaying, she glided into the entrance lobby.

Taking the glass Thomas offered, Miranda looked around uncertainly.

'Hey, partner,' Wade's voice came so softly under the babble of the newly arrived guests outside the room that only she had heard. He patted the empty space beside him.

Miranda shook her head. 'Estée will be back. I'll——' She looked for Thomas, but it seemed that he had joined Estée in welcoming the guests.

Jimmy, from floor level, glass to his lips, appeared to be oblivious to the proceedings, but the smile that rested against the crystal goblet's rim was both knowing and cryptic.

As Miranda hovered irresolutely, Wade's question hissed towards her. 'Who's the boss in our little arrangement?'

Miranda turned away, nose in the air in her attempt to squash the questioner, but hard fingers shot out, gripping her wrist and pulling her down.

'There isn't one,' she hissed back. 'We're equals. A partnership, strictly business.'

'Who pays whom?' Wade shot back.

He was right, but it was not in her to give in lightly. She made a face. 'Pulling rank, aren't you? It's not fair!'

He laughed, head back, eyes dancing. Miranda joined in his laughter, and when they came down to earth Jimmy was crouching in front of them. He looked from one to the other, stroking his beard.

'For a man who hates female fans,' he nodded at Wade, 'and a woman who's vowed never to fall at said man's feet,' with a nod at Miranda, 'you two are unbelievably chummy!'

'Strictly business, Jimmy,' Wade replied with a crooked smile. 'She's just said so.'

'Just as well, isn't it, seeing she's got a man of her own?' There was a strained silence. The joke was over—Jimmy's comment had been a timely reminder, for Miranda, at least.

The room was filling, the noise level rising. Someone almost knocked Jimmy flying and he straightened, moving away.

Bewildered, Miranda looked around. Wade caught her expression and his mouth curved. 'Wall to wall with people—that's how Estée likes it.'

A tray passed at nose level and Wade made a grab. 'Hey, Marie!'

'It's punch, Mr Bedford,' the girl closely resembling Dorothea told him.

He handed a glass to Miranda, who savoured the drink, feeling the need of it. The gentle yodelling music had been replaced by something with a beat, but even that was scarcely audible above the babble of voices.

'Hey, Tommy!' The high-pitched feminine voice had Miranda's eyes searching for the speaker. She found her, beside her fiancé. The face and the blonde hair were familiar; she had seen them in Thomas's collection of photographs.

And that girl had dared to call Thomas by the name he usually rejected fiercely? When would he turn on her, reprimanding her, correcting her angrily?

He did none of those things, instead smiling benignly at the speaker. Oh, heavens, Miranda thought, another complication! For Thomas to have tolerated Anita's use of the hated derivative of his name could only indicate that he had fallen for Anita Macfarland, and hard.

'Tommy,' Anita repeated, 'isn't that Wade Bedford over there? I've served him at the restaurant, but that's the nearest I've ever got. Oh, Tommy,' she begged, hanging on to his arm, 'lead me to him, please! I've been longing to meet him. He looks as fabulous in the flesh,' she drew out the word, 'as he does on the screen.'

Glancing at Wade, Miranda saw a muscle working in his cheek. His eyes had darkened, his teeth seeming to meet in a snap. If I hadn't already guessed, she thought, watching Anita pushing her way through the crush, I'd know now for certain how he would react if I were ever crazy enough to tell him I loved him.

'Mr Bedford?' Anita's hand came out, and Wade was too polite to ignore it. 'I'm a terrific fan of yours. I think you're fabulous! Sometimes I dream about you . . . but then I guess so do lots of women. I suppose I'm one of thousands, but just think, here you are in front of me, *for real* . . . I——'

'Hey there, everybody—food's being served!' Jimmy's voice was bellowing; it couldn't fail to be heard above the din. 'Come and get it!'

Wade rose as if he couldn't wait another minute to appease his hunger, but Miranda knew that it was Anita's declaration of undying adoration that was the cause of his sudden departure.

'Please excuse me,' he said coolly, nodding to Anita, Thomas and Miranda in turn, taking himself away and part of Miranda with him. He had classified *her, his business partner*, as just another 'hanger-on', and somewhere deep inside her there was a cry of pain.

CHAPTER NINE

IT WAS a long time later—hours, it seemed to Miranda—before she came even within sight, let alone touch, of Wade again.

The crowd had closed in—or had he deliberately clothed himself with it to keep any other possible lady 'fan' at bay, including one Miranda Palmer?

Only occasionally had she caught a glimpse of Thomas, and every time Anita had been at his side. Wade had continued—perhaps deliberately?—to ignore her own presence, so, to pacify herself, Miranda clutched at straws.

Had he assumed that Thomas had stayed with her? Maybe the crush had prevented him from seeing that almost every other male in the room, regardless of age, *except* himself and Thomas, had drifted purposefully over to her, pressing close, gazing into her eyes with earnestness—and definitely something more—until she politely moved away?

Estée's voice, pitched high, rose above the party babble. 'Hey, everybody, hide your faces . . . Thomas has been let loose with a video camera!'

Loudly, Jimmy laid claim to it. 'Get some good ones, Thomas!' he yelled, hands around his mouth for amplification. 'Then maybe you could use the result to blackmail these famous ladies and gentlemen all around us. Including me, of course.' He seized Estée and kissed her boisterously. She shrieked, but did not push him away.

Music drowned the cries of mock-horror at the appearance of the camera. The floor cleared miraculously for dancing, and Miranda's heart jumped as she spied Wade only a few feet away.

'Wade, Wade!' Anita pushed her way towards him. 'I know it's unconventional, but *please* would you dance with me? Just so I can boast to my friends at drama school?'

Wade's nostrils flared but, to Miranda's relief, he did not refuse. His hands came out and Anita went into them, not seeming to mind one bit that he held her at arm's length.

Anita talked the dance away, while Wade nodded occasionally, now and then even breaking into a smile. The music stopped and almost immediately started again.

Ready to continue, Anita watched, just a little disconcerted, as Wade bowed his thanks and left her, his strides taking him to Miranda's side. A contented sigh escaped Anita's smiling lips and she turned away, seeking another partner.

'Dance,' Wade commanded, swinging Miranda into action.

'It was good of you,' she remarked lightly, the blood in her veins in full spate, 'not to trample over Anita's dreams.'

He lifted a shoulder. 'This time, and in the special circumstances, I made an exception.'

A disruptive figure appeared on the dance-floor, video camera working full blast. Couples shouted, turned away, pretending to run for cover, joining in the general laughter. Thomas, Miranda thought affectionately, was helping to make the party go with a swing.

'Isn't it just great for our *business relationship*,' she pretended to joke, 'that I'm not one of your adoring fans flat on my face at your feet?'

'Which you vowed you would never be.'

'Correct. Never.' He could not see her crossed fingers resting on his shoulder.

'I breathe again. Our working partnership can
continue unthreatened.'

'Completely fireproof,' she agreed, feeling tears well
secretly and uselessly in her deepest being, 'hermetically
sealed from any emotion whatsoever. After all, as
Jimmy said, I've got a man of my own, haven't I?'

'Then I suggest,' Wade clipped, 'that you prise that
determined young woman from his side.'

Glancing over her shoulder, Miranda saw that Anita's
head was close to Thomas's as they studied the slowly
circling couples, apparently deciding between
themselves who was worthy of being filmed.

Miranda shrugged. 'I'm not worried.' And that
statement was truer than Wade would ever know.
'Thomas has already informed me that Anita's strictly a
career girl.'

Wade said nothing, but his arms, seeming to tire of
holding her in the conventional way, slid down to her
waist, encompassing it. 'Put your arms around my
shoulders, partner,' he said softly. 'You're still too far
away.'

Had he spoken those words to Estée, Miranda
wondered, as they had danced so closely that day on the
restaurant terrace?

The chandeliers above their heads had been
extinguished, the wall lights taking over, adding
romance and mystery to the atmosphere. Here in this
man's arms, Miranda thought she would faint with
happiness.

The music switched to the romantic, tantalising the
emotions. Wade pulled her closer still, the movement of
his body against hers, not to mention the elusive male
scent of him, sending her senses reeling.

Her body followed the rhythm and the sway, and,
when Wade's lips started caressing hers, parting them
and drawing from them a lingering kiss, she was caught
completely unawares.

Even though they had halted beside the revealing glow of a wall light, she found herself responding unreservedly to the sensation of pleasure and excitement his mouth was arousing. She couldn't help it, she was giving him kiss for intoxicating kiss, her taste-buds drowning in the wine from the forbidden fruit.

His lips trailed her cheek, his breath sweet on her sensitised skin. If he kissed her again, she would succumb to him entirely, and the world, not just Wade Bedford, would know just how deeply in love she was with him.

So, steeling herself for whatever trauma his reply to her question might cause, she asked, 'Who's Patti?'

Had his step faltered? Or was she over-sensitive to his every reaction? 'Patti? She's special, very special,' was his cut-off, keep-out answer.

Miranda's heart tripped and almost stopped. There had been affection as well as respect in his voice, and a kind of possessiveness in the words which he had chosen to describe the lady.

And that Miranda reflected, told her without any room for doubt the identity of Wade Bedford's true love. But, she agonised, had she really thought that such a *male* man as he was had gone through life pushing *all* women relentlessly to one side?

The party went boisterously on all around them.

Miranda groaned, her head seemed to be in two minds—whether to split or stay whole. And the alarm clock would not be silent, not even when she dived under the bedclothes. Not until her agitated finger reached out to still its raucous summons did it settle down quietly, having done its duty and its worst.

The party, after Wade's curt 'trespassers into my private life will be trampled underfoot' notice, had, for Miranda, lost its shine. She had thought she might as well find her jacket among the mêlée of outerwear on

Estée's bed, and slip out unnoticed.

Wade had disappeared into the crowd. The other male guests seemed to have decided that he had abandoned his bodyguard role, and made a beeline. As a consequence, Miranda found herself once again at the end of the scent trails followed by the male of the species.

To be surrounded by admiring men was, in a way, a sop to her injured pride, but it did nothing to fill the emptiness left behind by the man who, having bowed politely and formally, had left her stranded on the dance-floor. The kind of treatment, Miranda had reflected bitterly, that Wade seemed expert at meting out to anyone, not only women fans, who seemed to be in danger of treading where even angels wouldn't dare to go. She knew then exactly how Anita had felt.

Forcing herself to rise, she showered and dressed, wishing she had refused the glasses pressed on her by all those men who had hovered around her like moths around a flame. Except that all her warmth had deserted her, Wade having unknowingly taken it with him, and all the smiles that had afterwards decorated her face, and the laughter that had escaped her throat, had been forced and utterly false.

She breakfasted alone, having looked into Thomas's room and found it empty. Whether or not he had staggered back after the party, or had spent the night on Estée's floor, she could not tell, since his bed remained permanently unmade and his floor constantly littered with his belongings. Even Dorothea had given up trying to fight her way through the chaos to reach the bed in order to make it.

Of Wade that morning there was no sign. She did not even know whether he had returned after the party, and she certainly wasn't intending to peer into *his* room, she decided, to discover the answer.

One of Estée's friends had brought her home, Wade

having apparently asked him to do so. Thomas, at that time, had switched back to his own camera and was busy taking shots of anything that passed across his viewfinder.

Getting down to work, Miranda reacquainted herself with Wade's description of Patti. A few strokes of pencil across paper came to nothing. Frustrated, angry with her artistic self for letting her down yet again, she realised that, where Patti Burton was concerned, she was suffering from the same kind of creative block that had so troubled Wade.

Something—jealousy, perhaps, or plain despair?—was preventing her from visualising the woman. All she could gather from Wade's words was that Patti was young and intelligent, and apparently possessed brown hair and bright eyes—colour unspecified.

Sighing, Miranda took up a pen, but after a few attempts she threw it down. Head in hands, she heard the distant ring of the telephone.

Dorothea came hastening along the corridor. 'Oh, good, you are here, Miss Palmer. Mrs Faringdon is calling from Scotland. She wants Mr Bedford, but I cannot find him, so she is asking to speak to you.'

'Miranda, my dear!' Mrs Faringdon exclaimed. 'It's so pleasant to hear your voice again. How are things? I understand my nephew is out? You're getting on well, you two?'

'Our business arrangement is—er—going well, Mrs Faringdon.'

'A very diplomatic answer, dear. I'm aware that my nephew is not always the easiest of persons to get on with. By the way, I'm happy to be able to tell you that my sister has made wonderful progress in fighting off her health troubles.'

Miranda expressed her delight at the news.

'Which means,' Felicity Faringdon went on, 'that I

may soon be free to resume my work. Is there any chance, do you think, that Wade's book might be completed soon? In which case,' she continued in the absence of a reply from Miranda, 'would you be free to take up your position as my assistant again? That is, if you have no other plans, like becoming the artist you should really be? I would return to my house in London, of course, not to the chalet.'

The question set Miranda's thoughts in a whirl. How should she answer—turn the offer down flat, or hold on to it as a lifeline if everything else—including Wade's desire to write this book of his—should fail?

'It's very difficult . . . I'm afraid I really can't say yet, Mrs Faringdon. Only Wade knows how well his writing is going——'

'I quite understand. That's why I wanted to speak to him. Never mind, nothing is definite yet from this end. I just wanted to hear how the land lay, as it were, where you were concerned. Think about it, Miranda, won't you? And perhaps Wade will contact me himself some time.'

Back in her ski-room-studio, Miranda stared out at the mountains. She would never get around to climbing them, would she? And for her, the highest mountain of all, more daunting by far than the Matterhorn, than even Everest itself, was Wade Bedford, towering above her, his essence, his summit, forever out of her reach.

Time, she felt intuitively, was running out for her there. It wasn't just Mrs Faringdon's phone call; it was—oh, so many things. Her love for Wade, the way she had been tricking him, not to mention his aunt, his hatred, as he'd told her, of impostors—hadn't she been one of those from the moment she had met him?

'Enjoy the party?'

Miranda swung round, heart pounding. Wade leant against the table, arms folded. His dark sweater threw shadows upward to his unshaven face. Had he spent the night at Estée's too?

'Yes, thank you.'

'So lukewarm! You seemed happy enough to be surrounded by admiring males, laughing at their jokes, giving them the come-on with those eyes of yours.'

That she could not allow to pass. 'Oh, no, you've got it wrong. If I ever give that signal——'

'Which you do. That much I can tell you.'

'Then—then—it's purely unconscious . . .' *Did* she? To him? But how could she help herself, loving him as she did?

'I—I'm sorry if I do. Please overlook it. Maybe—er—I'm thinking of Thomas when it happens.'

His eyes narrowed. 'Ah, I wondered when his name would crop up. He neglected you badly, didn't he, yesterday evening?'

'He was having a ball trying out Jimmy's camera. He's never had the chance before to use one.'

Wade looked sceptical at her defensive attitude, her attempt to make excuses for Thomas's absence from her side, but he let the subject drop. 'You enjoyed the film show?' he asked casually.

'Yes, I did, thanks.'

In a quiet half-hour, with Jimmy's assistance and the use of Estée's television set, Thomas had shown the video shots he had taken during the evening.

Miranda smiled, recalling Jimmy's dry comments as she had floated by on the screen cradled in Wade's arms.

'Don't trust that snake in the grass, that cult figure who's got you in his clutches,' Jimmy had cracked. 'Silver-tongued and handsome as they come, but his treatment of the women in his life has to be seen to be believed. I should stick to good old Thomas—he's as open and honest as the day's long.'

'Hey, are you two engaged or something?' Anita's voice had asked, sounding distinctly put out.

'Yes, well—er—sort of.' Thomas had cleared his throat. 'Yes,' he had added, clearly remembering that his very presence there depended on it. 'Yes, we are.'

'Your aunt—she rang from Scotland,' Miranda told Wade now, thinking it advisable to change the subject. 'You were out——'

'Jogging round the block.'

'You—you stayed until the end last night?'

He smiled slightly. 'Estée's parties don't end, they just fade away. It's probably still going on.'

So that was where Thomas was!

'I phoned my aunt back, by the way.' Wade offered no further information on the subject. Straightening, hands sliding into his waistband, he asked, 'Free at the moment? Good. My brain's switched to its creative mode. The dam's burst and my mind's unblocked. I could dictate the torrent into my tape recorder, but I'd prefer you to take it down.' He looked around at the drawings—her own—with which she had adorned the bare walls. 'In here.'

It wasn't intended as a compliment, Miranda told herself firmly as she found her notepad—just that, as a human being, he considered that she was more receptive to his changes of mood and thought direction than a piece of mechanical equipment.

His writer's block had indeed disappeared. The words flowed, scene after horrifying scene coming alive, scrawling frightening pictures across Miranda's artistic vision, leaving her breathless and shocked.

If this was what he had been through, no wonder he had needed to recuperate from his physical injuries! But how, she wondered, would he ever recover from their impact on his mind?

Dictating session over, he nodded his thanks and went out without another word.

For some time Miranda stared after him, a kaleidoscope of images passing through her mind. She seized her sketchbook and picture after picture flowed from her hand. *Her* mind had become unblocked too, and as she worked a portrait appeared before her of a young woman with brown hair and laughing eyes—plus an integrity and intelligence so deep, she knew instinctively that they would reach down into Wade's very heart.

Mid-afternoon, Thomas wandered in, eyes heavy, face pale.

Preoccupied, Miranda glanced up. 'Hi.' She frowned, then laughed. 'Don't think I'm being unkind, will you?' she remarked. 'But you look, Thomas, as if you've been mauled by a baby tiger! Or,' she teased, 'may I call you *Tommy*?' He winced and held his head. 'Er—how's Anita?'

'Same as me, except she had to go to work, poor kid.'

'You like her, don't you?'

'She's OK.' He groaned. 'I need some sleep. See you around.' He turned at the door. 'You look perky. Wade Bedford anything to do with it?'

He was, and yet he wasn't, but Miranda had no intention of telling Thomas her secrets, so she shrugged her shoulders. 'Jealous?'

'Oh, my head!' moaned Thomas, changing the subject.

'I liked your efforts with the video camera.'

He brightened a little. 'Thanks.' His hand lifted and fell, and Miranda heard his door close quietly behind him.

He joined her for the evening meal, however, having apparently thrown off his hangover. Mr Bedford, Dorothea had announced, sent his apologies and was dining in his room, being busy working.

Soon afterwards Thomas announced his intention of going across to Estée's again. 'Or Jimmy's, I should say,' he added. 'Going to use his darkroom. I want to develop all those shots I took last night. OK with you?'

'Why should I object?' Miranda smiled. 'Burning the old midnight oil again?'

'Could be, who knows?' he answered enigmatically.

Wade, passing her studio some time later, caught a glimpse of her busy figure. He turned back, the doorway framing him. 'I don't expect you to work all hours just because my thoughts are in full flood. Take a break, partner.'

It hit Miranda then that she did indeed feel tired. Weariness made her drop her guard and she gazed at him, drinking in his strength, her artist's eye noting the firmness of his limbs, the span of his shoulders, the shaded stubbornness around his jawline. The woman in her reached out to the shadows around his eyes, the unusual pallor of his cheeks, making her want to run to him and stroke away his own fatigue.

His own eyes narrowed, speculation firming his features, and with a rush of colour to her cheeks she looked away.

'Good idea,' she murmured. 'I'm working late because, like you, I felt the creative urge.'

Wade had advanced softly and was beside her, startling her. Firm fingers lifted her face. 'Two of a kind. Whoever would have guessed I'd ever discover my female counterpart?'

'No, Wade,' she returned huskily, 'that I am not. I don't possess either your insight or your intellect. Nor do I have your courage, and your unflinching determination to get my message through no matter what the cost to myself.'

'You're talking,' he returned softly, and there was no doubt about the faintly warning note, 'like a fan, and you know what that means, lady.'

She jerked her chin away. 'Not true.' She pointed to his feet. 'Am I down there?'

'No, and you'd better never be.'

'I have been warned,' she replied, emphasising each word angrily. 'And have no fear, I shall heed it.'

Wade had gone and, needing the break he had advised, feeling also the urge to work off her anger against him for his subtle reproof, especially when she had truly meant every word, Miranda found a jacket and went for a walk.

The streets were quieter now, and she became aware of a change taking place in the temperature. It was sinking with the sun, but there were other signs. A heavy mist was descending and, in the premature darkness, lights came on all around.

The Matterhorn had disappeared, the mountain ranges with it. There was a rumble of thunder and Miranda shivered, wishing she had not ventured so far from the chalet. Turning, she made for home, the lights of all the hotels she passed made brighter by the gloom, giving out their own kind of reassurance.

Making it back, she shed her jacket and lingered in the living-room. Where was Wade? she wondered. Like Thomas, at Estée's place? Thunder rumbled and roared, echoing from the distant, invisible mountains. Lightning darted, affecting the lights. Even the trees and flowers moved agitatedly, the birds seeming worried, diving and swooping.

'Afraid of storms?'

The question made her jump, then shudder, her heart pounding. 'Wade! You frightened me.' Recovering, she answered, 'Normally, no. Just being alone, or I thought I was, in a strange house in a strange land. A sort of primitive reaction, I suppose.'

He joined her at the window, and his proximity, she found, was causing a greater storm inside her than the one outside. Her heart was racing now, and she could not prevent her eyes from glancing sideways, encountering a brooding expression, as if he were seeing

other places, hearing other sounds. Rain broke free of
the stormclouds, lashing against the windows.

She asked, half fearful of bringing him back too
precipitately to the present, like someone hesitating to
waken a sleepwalker, 'Your injuries—have they all
healed now?'

His eyes swung to her, although she wondered if it
was her he was seeing. 'More or less. There's still a little
pain and some stiffness, but they will go with time.'

So, she wondered, how long now before he felt the
urge to return to the work and the world he had left
behind? Was part of him straining to go back to the
danger inherent in his job? Was he longing to feel the
adrenalin rise once more as the challenge and the risks
increased?

'Have you finished work for the day?' she ventured in
the face of his sombre mood.

'If you're asking in a roundabout way whether I'll
need you to help me this side of midnight,' he smiled,
'the answer's no. Thanks.' It was a kind of dismissal,
despite the reasonableness of his tone.

'I'll go to bed, then. The storm isn't quite so bad
now.'

He nodded and returned to contemplating the
darkened land.

At the door, Miranda paused. She looked with
longing at the breadth and height of him silhouetted as
he was against the window. There was strength in every
line of him, even in his face, and she wanted to rush
back and tell him the truth, holding nothing back: that
she wasn't engaged to Thomas, never had been and
never would be, and that she loved another man—Wade
Bedford—so very much.

If she allowed herself such self-indulgence, for that
was all it would be, it would be the end of
everything—her work, her future, but most of all of her
acquaintance with Wade. The only time she would see

him again would be on the television screen, talking to millions.

It was in the early hours that Miranda became aware of the sound that had disturbed her. Fighting through to consciousness, she struggled with the bedcover and pushed it away, sitting on the side of the bed and listening.

All she heard was the distant rumble of thunder, the mountain ranges amplifying the boom. What, she wondered, should she do? Get back to sleep, she supposed. Then she heard the noise again. No thunder this—it was a human being in distress.

There was a cut-off shout, a warning to someone, a cascade of curses and invective. There was another cry, a low groan of anguish . . . Tearing out of the room, Miranda burst into Wade's bedroom and, in the light from the corridor, saw his half-covered figure, arms over his head, his face in the pillow. He seemed to be fighting for breath, drawing it in in an agonised spasm of pain.

'Patti,' he was moaning, 'get out, get away, find a doctor. Leave me, *leave me*! I—can—look—after—myself . . .'

His bare shoulders juddered like someone weeping dry tears, and filled with an inexpressible, dammed-up anger. His rib-cage expanded and contracted, the muscles in his back moving with it.

Face down, he kicked with his legs, and the sheet slithered away to reveal his powerful body, the back of his bulky calves, the sinewy columns of his thighs. His wounds, scattered over his left side, had almost healed, the scars remaining, livid yet and clear enough still to send shafts of empathetic pain through Miranda's trembling body.

The sight of Wade Bedford, dynamic and vigorous, full of courage and fight, laid low by the blows of circumstances and other people's wars, made her shake

with rage and a terrible resentment against the tricks
which fate had played on him . . . and a profound and
shattering shellburst of love.

His naked figure moved again in a long, slow shudder
of agony, and Miranda threw herself on to him, crying
out his name and jerking at his shoulders to drag him
out of his terrible, living nightmare.

After a few endless seconds the action seemed to have
succeeded. Wade lay still, his clawing hands on the
pillow slowly relaxing, the muscles in his limbs
loosening enough to let him slacken all over and slide
into something resembling sleep.

Miranda found that she was sobbing, dry, racking
sobs that shook her, but as his breathing deepened to
gain a normal, resting rhythm she breathed deeply too,
willing herself to be still while he lost himself in a sweet,
refreshing sleep.

Her hand felt for the sheet and she pulled it carefully
over them, the front of her body curved to the side of
his. Her arm was across him, her breath moving strands
of his hair as he lay, face turned from her. Her breasts
beneath the thin nightdress were pressed against him,
and she told herself she didn't care if he woke in the
morning and called her wanton and abandoned to be
where she was. She didn't care about anything now
except that Wade should stay free of haunting terror,
calmed and relaxed in her arms.

His breath fanned her mouth, and she realised that he
had turned his head towards her on the pillow. His eyes
fluttered open and he stared at her face.

Her words tumbled out as a form of self-defence.
'You were having a terrible nightmare. You called out,
so I came.' His stare did not waver. 'It was awful,
Wade, you were living it all again. It—it was probably
making yourself remember it for the book, then
dictating it . . .'

He gazed at her as if he were still wrapped in a dream.

Speaking in a hoarse whisper, she said, 'You were calling to Patti. Wade——' it was vital that he should know without any possible doubt, 'I'm not Patti. I'm Miranda.' She shook his arm a little. 'Do you hear?'

'I hear.' A small smile played round his mouth. 'You're the girl who almost told me she——'

'No!' Her hand went across his mouth. 'It was infatuation, momentary and passing—we agreed on that. Not love——' She caught her breath as his fingers imprisoned her wrist, pressing her palm against his lips.

'Thanks,' he muttered to the sensitive centre of her hand, 'for rescuing me from my nightmare. I should have bad dreams every night, then I might have you for company——'

'It was no joke, Wade. It was terrible! You really scared me, the way you were. I had to help you somehow.'

'You couldn't have chosen a better way,' he responded huskily, turning fully to face her. The sheet was still across them, but she could feel the taut strength of his thighs and the thrusting firmness of his hips.

As his body came to life next to hers, she realised that her body was arousing his. 'I suspect,' he said thickly, 'that you may not know what you're doing to me.'

'Oh, Wade, I——' She shook her head wildly, instinct telling her to pull away and go, even as her longing, inextricably mixed with the heat of desire which she had never experienced before, tugged her towards him.

His mouth came down on hers, drawing the taste of her into him, taking her very breath into his lungs. The action held an intimacy of its own and her lips parted involuntarily, allowing him deeper access.

From the total feel of his nakedness against hers, she realised he had removed her nightdress. She made to put a distance between them. She had to take some action to bring to a halt this perilous but increasingly irresistible journey into Wade Bedford's magic, magnetic orbit . . .

only to be spun off afterwards into space, unwanted by him and discarded for the rest of her life.

Her skin quivering against his hard flesh was almost her undoing, her femininity flowering to fullness as his hands coaxed and incited her to a feverish need.

He was murmuring endearments and she tried to hear the words so that she could treasure them in the years to come. But they were spoken against her heated skin and she could not make them out.

Her own lips parted to tell him, whispering so softly that he wouldn't hear, how much she loved him. Even as she took a breath to speak, a shattering thought entered her mind, causing her to close her lips and keep her secret. *Was he making love to her believing she was Patti?* No matter what effect he was having on her, she must force herself to face that possibility.

His lips savouring her breasts, his tongue circling their taut pink points, his trailing fingertips caressing her most intimate places, her ecstatic response and gasps of breath, were all conspiring to take them beyond the point of no return.

'No, no, you must stop!' Was it her voice crying out?

Wade did not seem to hear as he impelled her on to her back, and part of her delighted in the strength of his hands manipulating her. But that deep-down instinct raised its voice until her ears rang with its command . . . Stop him now, do you understand? You would have to tell him the truth—that you're not the engaged woman he believes you to be. *He would hate you then, because he hates impostors.*

'Thomas, oh, Thomas . . .' The words came from a secret hiding-place, hanging on the air, hovering like a terrible black cloud above them.

Miranda closed her eyes, feeling the sudden grasp of his angry hands just before they released her, feeling the rush of cold air as his body lifted from hers. Alone in the bed, for a few despairing seconds she hid her face in the pillow.

Then, dragging herself upright, standing on the tufted rug, she groped for her nightgown, pulling it on. His back was to her as he stared, hands on hips and clothed in a robe, into the mountainous darkness beyond the windows.

'Wade?' she whispered. 'I'm sorry.' Head high, body rigid, he made no response.

'Do you mind, Miranda,' queried Thomas, 'if I quit?'

Her heart jolted. 'You mean from our engagement?'

'Well, I really meant go home. I've enquired about flights, and there's one available the day after tomorrow.'

'Even though it means leaving Anita behind? You like her, don't you?'

He fidgeted with one of his photographic gadgets. 'She's OK. Her father's in advertising, and she said he might be able to help me with a vacation job. And that might lead to something more permanent when I finish my course. She's leaving soon too,' he added, as if it were of little consequence.

Miranda was not deceived, but she kept her smile to herself. 'That's just great. Thomas?' He looked up. 'Do you mind if we keep this going,' she held out the ring he was supposed to have given her, 'for a bit longer? Until I get back too?'

His shoulders lifted and fell. 'Because of your job here? OK by me. Just as long as I can tell Anita the truth—in strictest confidence, of course.'

'Of course. I hope you've enjoyed your time in these parts.'

He brightened considerably. 'It's been great, Miranda. Thanks a lot.' He leaned forward and kissed her, on the mouth, a sweet if meaningless kiss.

Someone passed the door of Thomas's room. Miranda knew that tread by heart. Wade would have to choose that moment, she thought, her heart taking a dive. Was he on his way to the ski-room? Running to the door, she saw him turn into it. 'See you around,' she said to Thomas, and hurried after Wade.

'I'm sorry it's in such a——' He was looking at her sketch of Patti. 'Oh, that,' she commented uncomfortably, 'it was the best I could do in the circumstances.'

Wade was frowning. 'Have you ever seen her?'

'Patti Burton?' She shook her head. 'How could I?'

'A camera couldn't have made a better job of her likeness.' The words held praise, but the voice that had spoken them was icy cold. Miranda shivered inside, feeling as if she were marooned in a storm on one of those mountains, cut off from civilisation itself.

'Thank you,' she said, trying a smile to bridge the terrible chasm that had opened up between them, but he might just as well have been on the summit of the Matterhorn, so remote and unapproachable was he.

He replaced the sketch and went to the door.

'Do you need me for dictation?' If he did, Miranda reasoned, it would at least imply that there was still room for her in his life, even it if was on a purely commercial basis.

'Thank you, no.' His mask of a face, his cool detachment cut into her. 'I'm taking a break. When I need your secretarial services again, I'll let you know.' It was a dismissal arising starkly out of that business arrangement they had, and its effect on her was devastating.

'Wade!' His name was torn from her like an echoing cry in the white wilderness of the mountain ranges. 'I'm not engaged to Thomas . . .' Oh, heavens, she thought, did I really speak those words?

The ferocity of his response made her cringe as if she were being attacked by a mountain lion. 'You're trying to tell me you've thrown him aside,' he rasped, each word inflicting its own wound, 'broken your engagement to him on the strength of one erotic tussle on the bed, one that *you* initiated, with the cult figure Wade Bedford? You've done that to Thomas?'

His eyes glittered like pieces of ice, his tone froze her blood. I came to you in the night, she tried to say, because you were being torn apart by that terrible nightmare. I wanted to help you, bring you back to reality and out of those dreadful dreams . . .

'You're standing there,' he rasped, giving her no chance to clear herself, 'cold-bloodedly rejoicing—yes,' seeing her flinch, 'I mean cold-bloodedly, after all those declarations you've made about never "falling at my feet", and about "never losing your heart to me", and so on, with monotonous regularity, so I repeat—cold-bloodedly rejoicing in the fact that you've succeeded where all those other women failed? That you, Miranda Palmer, managed to get that newsreel idol—almost—to bed you? You're attaching significance to what in a man is a purely reflex action?' He walked towards her, head slightly lowered, teeth gritted.

'Grow up, Miranda. You practically threw yourself at me, getting into my bed, putting your arms around me, all of which you can't deny.' She could, but again it was obvious that he didn't want to know. His lip curled. 'I do believe,' he sneered, 'that you've actually fooled yourself into thinking that those kisses we've on occasion exchanged, that that slightly lurid episode on the bed,' he gestured to the upper storey, 'held as much meaning for me as they appeared, quite misguidedly, to have had for you?'

Shaking fingers covered her trembling lips. She wanted to speak, to defend herself, but no words would come.

'Tell me,' he sneered, 'what exactly were you after? A wild fling before marriage?'

'No, I——'

'What did become plain in the course of our . . . acquaintance was that you were a woman of flexible morals. That you had every intention, probably in view of Thomas's absences abroad, of making yours a "free" marriage. So I knew that, in view of all you'd said, I could make love to you knowing you wouldn't take it seriously.' He made an angry sound in his throat. 'Go back to that young man, Miranda. *He's* straightforward and honest.' Implying, she thought miserably, that I'm not.

Could he, she wondered, wishing her lip would stop its trembling, have ground her pride more thoroughly into the dust? Told her more decisively, and derisively, what he thought of her? Informed her more clearly just how very little she meant to him?

How could she tell him now—and expect him to believe her—that her cry to Thomas had been the only course left open to her as a means of protecting herself from the lifetime of regret that would have stretched ahead when that most intimate of acts between them was over?

Wade's eyes were on her hands, watching her movements as she unconsciously twisted the mock engagement ring. 'So who were you trying to fool?' he accused angrily. 'You're still wearing Thomas's ring.'

In the distance, the telephone shrilled. Wade swung away, making for the exercise-room where there was a telephone extension.

'Who?' Miranda heard him ask, his expectations seeming to rise. 'Patti? My dear, I'm delighted to hear from you!' He listened. 'Come here to finish your convalescence? You'd be as welcome as the sun in the sky. Tomorrow? I'll meet you at the airport. Yes, Geneva. I know it's some distance, but what the hell. It's worth the drive to see you all the sooner.'

Patti Burton, the lady who, Wade had said, was so 'special' and who plainly meant the world to him, was coming to stay. But it had been the tenderness and concern and, Miranda forced herself to face it, deep affection in his voice that had told her, without any lingering trace of doubt, the identity of the holder, the keeper forever, of Wade Bedford's heart.

CHAPTER TEN

MIRANDA sealed the package carefully, addressing it to Mrs Faringdon's sister's house in Scotland.

Dear Mrs Faringdon, Thomas and I have no intention of getting married, so I am returning the ring you very kindly lent us. Thank you for that. I enjoyed working with you, and I hope that one day you will find another secretary, one preferably who has no secret ambition to fulfil herself as an artist!

Miranda had added a few words regarding Mrs Faringdon's own affairs, and wishing her sister a speedy and complete recovery. Taking the package, she walked to the nearby parade of shops to post it. So ends, she thought, walking back, an unforgettable interlude. She had cried no tears, they were locked inside her like an ache for which there was no known medication.

Two months had passed since she and Thomas, travelling together, had left Switzerland, for Miranda two months of pain and unrelenting loneliness. The moment Wade had left for Geneva, she had packed her belongings, leaving a note for him on his return.

I'm going home. I think this is best for all concerned. You probably won't want my illustrations, but I've left them in my room in a folder. Do what you like with them, throw them away if you want. I've enjoyed working with you, and I would like to wish you, and your book when finished, every success.

Penny was coming, so Miranda tidied the living-room and got out her sketchbook, but that was the wrong thing to do. It was filled with drawings—of Wade, of the mountains, of chalets and people and Wade again.

To escape from her thoughts, she switched on the television, watching it without much interest.

'Miranda!' Penny exclaimed, breezing in after ringing. 'What's on the telly? Hey, these drawings are great. You were good before, but I think you're even better now. Thomas sends his love. Sorry,' as Miranda winced, 'not real love—you know what I mean? He's crazy about Anita, did you know that?'

'I guessed. Her father's in advertising, isn't he?'

Penny laughed. 'You mean it's cupboard love?' She threw her jacket aside and joined Miranda on the sofa. She had been to Miranda's place many times. 'What you're saying is that Anita's dad might help him up the career ladder? I don't know about that, but,' she frowned, 'there's someone giving him chances. He won't tell me who, he says, in case it changes his luck.'

In the background, the television played to an inattentive audience.

Miranda leaned back, closed her eyes. 'Let me take a guess. Estée Adams, maybe, television producer. She's got good contacts. Or perhaps it's Jimmy—James Haverson,' Miranda explained. 'Top man of Spartacus International, publishers of newspapers, magazines, books——'

'You don't say!' Penny's mouth sprang wide open. 'No wonder my dear brother's been so pleased with himself since he came back! The people he's been mixing with! Not to mention——'

'Our tame screen idol, Wade Bedford.'

'I don't know why you're so bitter about the man, Miranda. What harm's he done you? From what you say, he did his best to give you a break by asking you to illustrate his book.'

Miranda had told Penny nothing of her feelings for Wade, of their curious affair that was not an affair. So she could not explain to Penny now that sarcasm had been the only weapon she had found with which to deal with the recurring dream of being in Wade's arms; the golden memories that gave pain instead of pleasure; the torment of being cut off from him, with neither phone call nor letter, even expressed in strictly business terms, to make the agony of being parted from him easier to bear.

'I admit he did that,' she answered with a sigh, 'but it all came to nothing. Work-wise, I'm back where I started.'

In the silence that followed, they idly watched the early evening news. Suddenly Penny's arm shot out, finger pointing.

'There he is,' she breathed, 'your Wade Bedford!'

'Not mine,' Miranda answered fiercely, but her eyes studied him from top to toe, her ears eager for his every word.

So he had gone back to work, as he'd said he would, back to the danger he seemed to thrive on. The shock of seeing him again told her how far she still had to travel along the road to a complete exorcism of him from her emotions.

He wore dark trousers which were creased and dusty, and a white open-necked shirt. His black hair bore a layer of dust too, and his jaw and chin a fine dark shadow. His brave and handsome face, his lean figure so vulnerable as machine-guns stuttered and bombs erupted all around him, his courageous and utterly selfless stance amid the man-made chaos, turned Miranda's heart over and over, making her shake with fear on his behalf.

He delivered his report in the unemotional tones which he had made his own, but the words he spoke lit fires of shock and outrage in the imaginations of his listeners. Someone in battledress had a gun trained on him, but Wade did not know.

How could he know, Miranda agonised, her teeth almost chattering for him, when he faced the camera and the fighter was crouched behind him? She was shaking with fear at the thought of the almost certain death that was awaiting him, and the room started to spin.

The next news item flashed on and Wade vanished from the screen. All Miranda's fears, all her vain and bitter love for the man behind that bold and handsome image gathered like a great roaring wave and crashed on the desolate and lonely shore of her mind.

'Whew,' said Penny, 'that was a close thing! Ah,' sympathetically as Miranda's hands went to her pale cheeks, 'I see it all now. No need to say a word.'

But it was only when Penny had gone that Miranda, for the first time since her return, let the suppressed tears come, giving way to her unhappiness and grief.

Two days later a telephone call set her thoughts in a turmoil.

'Miss Palmer?' the caller asked. 'Spartacus here.'

'S-Spartacus International?' The voice was not that of Jimmy Haverson. How could it be? He was the top man. He wouldn't be calling *her*, would he?

'The same. Book publishing division. Bob Parker's the name—editorial director. We're handling Wade Bedford's book——'

'But——' He hasn't finished it, Miranda was going to say. Or had he? Two months was a long time. Perhaps Patti, the lady he loved, had helped him. But Wade was abroad now. Hadn't she seen him on screen only a couple of days ago? He was still *living* his book, wasn't he, so how could he have completed it?

'Yes?' she added encouragingly, telling her thumping heart to take it easy.

'As you're his illustrator, Miss Palmer, we would very

much like to meet you—you know, a general editorial
discussion. Later on, we'll need to talk to you regarding
layout, format and so on. Then lunch. We're very
pleased with your work and we would enjoy meeting
you. How's your diary for possible dates?'

It's empty, she almost said, blank pages from here to
eternity. 'We-ell——' she hoped she was giving the
impression of turning pages.

'How about the day after tomorrow?'

'Oh——' Miranda tamed her gasp into a thoughtful
intake of breath, 'I think I could manage that.' Time
decided upon, call ended, she sank into a chair and
hugged herself. As an artist, was she on her way at last?

Entering the sky-high Spartacus building with its
façade of row on row of tinted glass, its uniformed
doorkeeper, his challenge softening into a welcoming
smile as she said her name and that of the man she had
come to see, she felt she should pinch herself to make
sure it wasn't all a dream.

Bob Parker, late thirties, brown-haired, busy-
looking, extended a firm and welcoming hand. No, he
said, the book wasn't yet finished, but Wade had made
vague promises to get on with it as soon as
circumstances allowed.

The discussion was invigorating and enlightening, the
members of the art department accepting Miranda's
inexperience in the field of book illustration, but
complimenting her on her quick grasp of the
technicalities.

As they left, Miranda disappeared to powder her nose
and to try and tone down the high colour the excitement
of the morning had put into her cheeks.

Returning to Bob Parker's office, she almost
collapsed with astonishment. Coming towards her,
smiling broadly, hand outstretched, was James
Haverson, chairman of Spartacus International.

'Oh, Jimmy,' she gasped, 'I'm so glad to see you!'

His arms enveloped her and his bearded kiss tingled on her cheek.

'You never did say goodbye, did you?' he chided gently. 'There was one furious author and journalist left behind who, for a day or two, behaved like an animal deprived of its food.'

'Oh, but, Jimmy——' Miranda pulled away. He had Patti, she almost said, then remembered protocol, not to mention his status. 'Er—Mr Haverson, I mean.'

'Hey, Miranda, all my friends call me Jimmy. You know that.'

'Yes, but——' She surveyed the length of him, his tailored clothes, his hair and beard combed to perfection, and remembered his penchant for the floor as the most comfortable place to sit.

Jimmy looked at his watch. 'Time for that meal we're sharing. Ready, Bob?'

'I've got an agent to see, Mr Haverson, so I left myself out of the lunch booking. I didn't think you'd mind.'

'You just carry on, Bob.' Jimmy took Miranda's arm. 'This way, lady.' Part way down the corridor, he pushed at a door. 'Welcome to my sanctum. Plenty of chairs—pity!' He smiled. 'I'd much prefer to recline on the floor. Remember?'

'Oh, Jimmy, I'll never forget.' Miranda's smile faded. There were other reasons why that happy interlude in Switzerland would remain for ever in her mind. One other reason, to be exact. She looked around. 'You're—you're very important, aren't you?'

He laughed. 'That's a relative term, Miranda. Out in the great wide world, even the chairman of a company's reduced to size. I——'

The door behind Miranda opened and Jimmy stared over her head, smiling strangely. Had Estée come, having returned from Switzerland too? His hand on her shoulder, he turned her, holding her firmly as a spasm jolted her body. 'Hey there, relax, Miranda,' he said softly, glancing at her white face. 'Hi, Wade. Welcome back.'

Wade's eyes were on the girl Jimmy held, but those eyes were drained of expression. Jimmy let his arm fall away, sensing that Miranda was over the shock.

Wade's eyes wandered, noting the neatness of her dark suit, the silver sheen of her contrasting blouse, its tie neck softening the impact of the businesslike outfit. Around her neck she wore a double row of wooden beads, craftsman-made and hand-turned, while her dangling crafted earrings were a perfect match.

He inclined his head, unsmiling. 'Miranda.'

If we'd been sworn enemies, she thought, his greeting couldn't have been less friendly!

'H-how is it that you're here?' she stammered. 'I saw you on television—the other night.' She could only manage short phrases, her mind was spinning like a top. 'There was a gun . . . behind you . . . trained on you. I thought—I really thought you might be killed.' Her voice caught in her throat.

'This time,' Jimmy commented drily, 'he dodged the bullets. Right, pal?'

'Right, Jimmy. The man behind the gun was a lousy shot.'

'How can you be so flippant,' Miranda protested passionately, 'about such a precious commodity as your own life?'

Wade's eyes were hooded at her outburst, his answer downbeat and dry. 'It goes with the job. Did I forget to tell you?'

Did he need to be so cold? she agonised, taking in the length and breadth of him, his formal suit and conventional tie turning him into the stranger he was pretending to be. This was a very different man from the one she had known and grown to love among those mountains, and she despaired of ever seeing again that dark-eyed, demanding lover who had—almost—made her his.

'I flew back yesterday,' Wade told her briskly, then drew back his cuff with something near to impatience. His watch, catching down the dark hairs, was gold. Of course it had to be, Miranda thought, bitterness rearing its head again.

Cult figure war reporter had to impress his adoring fans with flashy possessions, hadn't he? Well, she thought, how else but by cynicism could she protect herself from this twisting pain inside her which the mere sight of him created? So cold and distant—and so fine-looking too?

'Come on, you two,' Jimmy said sharply, 'break it up! Life's too short for arguments, even silent ones. A glass or two of wine inside you both will do wonders.'

'How's Thomas?' asked Jimmy when they were settled at their table in the busy restaurant a cab-drive away. There seemed to be an impish glint in his eye.

'He's fine,' answered Miranda, feeling herself compelled to add for honesty's sake, 'or so I'm told.'

'Ah,' said Jimmy, stroking his beard. 'I see you're not wearing his ring.'

It wasn't his ring. The words so nearly escaped, but she managed to imprison them just in time. Where Wade's opinion of her was concerned, which for some reason seemed to have reached a low ebb, a confession now of the truth about herself and Thomas would have made that opinion sink without trace.

There was silence for some time, in which Miranda played nervously with the cutlery, and Wade looked around him with studied indifference. Jimmy grew increasingly fidgety.

'Look,' he declared at last, 'snap out of it, you two. I brought you together because I want your finished book in our hands, Wade, and your illustrations, Miranda, completed and tied in with the script. Or,' and it was James Haverson talking, not Jimmy any more, 'have you, Miranda, got yourself such a good job in the art world, you're no longer interested in this partnership of yours with Wade?'

Miranda shook her head slowly. 'No art job, just temporary secretarial assignments.'

'You're telling me that with your ability, lady, you're still a secretary?'

She lifted her shoulders. Wade too was looking at her now, keenly, faintly puzzled.

'What about you, Wade?' Jimmy queried.

'Me? I'm thinking of abandoning the book.'

'Oh, but——' Miranda began, but Jimmy broke in,

'For pity's sake, man, why? From what I've read so far, it looks set to be a bestseller.'

The waiter appeared, serving the meal, and Jimmy simmered down, after which the conversation became general. Coffee finished, Jimmy pushed back his chair.

'If you two will excuse me,' he rose from his seat, taking his companions by surprise, 'I'm chairing a conference in twenty minutes. Did I forget to tell you?' Jimmy's smile, as he looked from one to the other, held a hint of mischief.

Wade looked like thunder. 'I'll get you for this, Haverson,' he muttered darkly, but Jimmy merely grinned in response.

'It's over to you, pal,' he commented, pushing in his chair. 'And remember the deadline I've set for your masterpiece to appear, in all its glory, on my desk.'

'I make no promises,' growled Wade, adding casually, 'Remember me to Estée.'

'I will. We're legalising things, did I tell you?'

'That's just great!' exclaimed Miranda, although Wade remained unmoved. But then he would, wouldn't he? Miranda thought. As I now know, it's Patti he's loved all this time. Against her, no woman, not even Estée Adams, stood a chance.

Jimmy kissed Miranda's cheek, whispering loudly, 'Take the advice of an old friend. Come off your high horse, girl . . . and pull *him* down with you. As I know by experience, it's much more comfortable at floor level.'

Miranda smiled reminiscently, but Wade's sense of humour seemed to have gone underground. A grim kind of silence followed Jimmy's departure. 'How's Patti?' Miranda asked, in an attempt to establish some kind of contact.

'Patti? She's fine.' His eyes clashed sardonically with hers. 'Or so I'm told.'

Miranda recognised her own words regarding Thomas, although she reasoned that Wade's uncertainty must have arisen through his having been abroad, and therefore not seeing Patti for some time.

Wade looked around him. Was he, Miranda wondered despondently, seeking some way of ridding himself of her company?

'I'll see you home,' he said stiffly.

Which was surely the signal she'd been dreading—that their time together was coming to an end. The reunion she had dreamed about, of running into his opened arms and being swept off her feet and into his life until the end of time . . . This hadn't been a dream, more of a nightmare. It certainly couldn't have been more of a fiasco if it had tried.

She was crying deep down, but her tone was crisp as she answered, 'There's no need, thank you. I can get a taxi——'

'I'll see you home,' he repeated grimly.

Affecting a sigh of resignation, Miranda followed him out, standing beside him as he hailed a cab, then preceding him into it.

'Is this the place, miss?' the driver asked, drawing up at a block of flats in the outer suburbs.

'Yes, thanks.' Getting out, Miranda raked in her

purse, assuming Wade would be returning the way he had come.

A hand on her arm stilled her action, notes were exchanged and she was left with Wade beside her, the taxi a speck in the distance.

She started to protest that he needn't have stayed, but Wade cut in sharply, 'We have to talk. As Jimmy said, things are becoming urgent.'

In his impeccably cut suit, with his height and his intimidating presence, he seemed to fill the living-room. On the television screen he always seemed larger than life. Yet here he was, dwarfing that screen, and she had only to reach out and he would be there, stinging the nerves of her fingers, electrifying her body.

Although she had to face it, in reality she was no nearer to him than when he had been a fleeting, unreachable image in front of her eyes. Like the Matterhorn, that glorious mountain she had seen every day of her stay at the chalet, he was for her remote and unconquerable, and always would be.

'Please,' she gestured to a low chair, remembering his liking for such seats in his Swiss chalet, 'make yourself comfortable.'

It seemed that the stranger he had become did not lounge carelessly, legs outstretched. This businessman she was entertaining preferred the other, straighter seat. Which put her at a disadvantage, since in the chair he had refused she found herself having to gaze up at him, while he from his vantage-point was able to look down on her.

'Would you like a drink?'

'Thank you, no.'

A conversational dead end. What now? Miranda wondered helplessly. Removing her jacket, she found him watching her every movement, which sent her entire nervous system into a spin.

'Was it——' she moistened her lips, 'was it your

absence abroad that prevented you from finishing your book?'

'No. Oh, no. You see,' his lips tightened, 'a vital ingredient was missing.'

'But—but Patti was there.'

'What about Patti?' She was so 'special', was she, that he didn't even want to discuss her?

Restlessly Wade got to his feet, pacing the room, swinging round to return. He removed his jacket as if it were doing him an injury, and flung it down. It flew outward as he did so, catching one of Miranda's crystal ornaments. As it fell from the shelf, she made a dive, crying, 'Oh, no, please don't break!'

At the same time Wade lunged to intercept its fall, colliding disastrously with her. The crystal swan, minutely faceted to catch and reflect the light, went on its perilous journey, crashing down and smashing to pieces on the tiled surround of the built-in electric fire.

Aghast, Miranda stared at the sparkling fragments. Something precious was gone from her life, something she loved. It seemed so symbolic, like her relationship, no matter how tenuous it had been, with the man who now stood beside her, separate and apart, despite the fact that inwardly he was an indivisible and indispensable part of her. Yet, after this discussion, he would go his own way and she hers.

'I'll buy you another.'

'No, no, it doesn't matter.' But it did, it mattered terribly, it twisted her insides like a knife being turned. She took a gasp to steady herself, but it turned into a shudder and she burst into tears.

'E-excuse me,' she muttered, making for the sanctuary of her bedroom, but Wade caught and held her, putting her head to his shoulder. It felt wonderful to be so near to him again—but something was wrong. His hold was loose and impassive, and as the outburst subsided he released her and walked away. She knew

why, didn't she? Patti was on his mind and she,
Miranda, had embarrassed him with the emotional
storm she had unleashed all over him. *Like an
infatuated fan, she'd committed the unforgivable sin of
falling at his feet . . .*

Drying her eyes, she breathed more steadily,
murmuring an apology. Wade stared at a framed
painting of the Welsh mountains, one of several of her
own that she had hung around the flat. Was it, perhaps,
reminding him of those other great mountain ranges
they had both left behind?

'Why the *hell*,' he swung round violently, speaking
through his teeth, 'did you pack up and go?' His eyes
were as dark and threatening as those stormclouds had
been over the chalet in the middle of his nightmare.
'How in heaven's name did you expect me to be able to
write my book without you there?'

How could she say, I went because I was superfluous
to your requirements? Patti Burton was joining you,
and she's the one you love. You wouldn't have wanted
me around.

'So—so you missed my professional help,' she
improvised instead, 'you needed those illustrations I'd
promised to supply as part of our business arrangement.
If it means that much to you,' she added flatly, rolling
her damp handkerchief into a ball, 'I'll do the work you
want, and Jimmy wants, and Spartacus International
book publishing division wants——'

In one stride he confronted her, gripping her
shoulders and giving her a shake. Jaw thrust forward,
he snapped, 'Will you cut out the sarcasm?' Her tear-
stained face lifted to his, a rogue sob shook her slender
frame. 'Will——' He stared into her brimming eyes and
his breath seemed to trip itself up.

'You can keep your pity!' she cried. 'It's infatuation
I'm suffering from, that's all. We agreed on that in
Switzerland, remember? I'm a fan, a worshipper at the

feet of the great Wade Bedford . . .'

He hunched her shoulders and placed his mouth on hers. Miranda struggled, freeing herself. 'It's not love that's killing me inside, it's hero-worship . . . Wade, no!' If he kissed her now, it would be the end. He'd guess, he'd realise . . .

She was in his arms and he was murmuring, 'There's a woman I want, I woman I need . . . *This* woman, no other.' He held her away. 'Don't you understand? *You* were the missing ingredient. Without you there, I couldn't produce a single bloody word. Can't you comprehend?'

'But—Patti?' she queried, frowning. 'She's special, you said.'

'You want to know about Patti? Sure she's special. I'll tell you why. She's a friend, more important, a colleague. You see,' he kept his arms tightly around her, 'the day I was shot, she was with me. She's a war reporter too. I got injured first, then she was in the firing line and a bullet got her hand.'

He was silent for a few moments, staring back in time. 'They went to her aid but not mine. She shouted that we were lovers, which we weren't, and she couldn't live without me, which she could. So, incredibly, they took pity on us both. We woke up in hospital. Patti kept her hand, thank heavens, and—the rest of the story you know.'

'So if it hadn't been for Patti—yes.' Miranda whispered, cheeks pale, 'I agree, she's very special.'

Wade searched her face, looked the length of her, then up again, as if only in her eyes could he see what he was seeking. 'Has no one ever told you,' he growled, 'what hell it is for a man to be without the woman he needs more than he needs the oxygen he breathes, the food he eats to stay alive?'

He pulled her to him, his cheek against her hair, his length pressed to hers.

'Tell me what you're saying,' she demanded, fighting against the wild delight that shone like a brilliant sun reappearing after a devastating storm. 'Tell me who it is you're talking about. Is it Patti, after all? She stayed with you at the chalet, didn't she? Am I really a substitute for her, are you using me to ease your frustrations because you had to leave her behind in Switzerland?'

'Oh, yes,' he murmured against the curve of her throat, making her shiver at the caressing touch of his lips, 'I'm using you to ease my frustrations.'

She tried to struggle free, but he held her easily, mocking her vain efforts.

'The frustrations I've been enduring when I've tried to live without you—not Patti, not Estée, but you, every moment of my absence abroad. You've driven me mad in the flesh, and you've almost driven me crazy in my dreams.'

She, Miranda, was the woman he'd been talking about? The joy of it made her want to laugh and cry all at once.

'In my dreams,' he went on, 'you were in my arms, I could touch you and make love to you, then you'd turn to shadow and disappear, going back to a ghostly figure who beckoned while you ran.'

His fingers went to the buttons of her blouse, but her hand went to cover his. 'Wade, I must tell you——'

'Not now,' he muttered against her lips. His fingers found their way through to the curves of her breasts, stroking and moulding. 'I've waited weeks, I'm not waiting any longer.' He paused in his caressing. 'Take it or leave it.'

'I—I take it, Wade,' she whispered, delight in her eyes and joy in her heart.

He lifted her and then they were in her bedroom. A quivering sensation crept over her skin as the vibrations of him were picked up by her body's antennae. As he slowly undressed her, kissing each fresh area of tingling skin as it glowed pink and white beneath his caressing eyes, the pleasure of his touch was exquisite. With each second that passed, her sensations were heightened, and then she was naked before him.

He stroked every part of her, then lowered her to the bed. Eyes never leaving her, he quickly discarded his clothes, and Miranda looked with loving admiration at his breadth and strength, his virile masculinity.

He came down beside her, and she found her hands running over his shoulders and down his arms, stroking, then kissing the scars and indentations the bullets had made and which still persisted.

His fingers caught her chin and lifted her mouth higher, the better to imprison it with his, drinking from the well of her, taking her essence, her very self into him. Under his caressing touch her body leapt to life, her need of him and her love for him intertwining until they were both indistinguishable from each other. She only knew that every inch of her flesh throbbed with the passion he was arousing, causing an ache to build up inside her that only he could cure.

She arched under the caress of his lips on her breasts, hearing him murmur, 'My love, you're like cool liquid to me after a trek through an endless, waterless desert.' Then he made a pathway for himself into her warm, pulsating softness, hesitating briefly, but letting nothing intrude upon their oneness. A cry of pure joy was wrenched from her as together they reached a shuddering pinnacle of delight.

Some time later, Wade stirred. 'How come, my love,' gently he nipped her ear, 'you've remained untouched until now?' He smiled into her eyes, the kind of smile, she thought, that would turn his fans' knees to water. 'After all, an engaged woman these days——'

'It was my choice. And—and I wasn't——' She couldn't delay any longer and braced herself for his fury and rejection. 'Wade, there's something I have to tell you. About Thomas.'

A shadow darkened his eyes. Taking a steadying breath, she confessed, 'I—I never was engaged to him. Your aunt made it a condition of her giving me the job that I had a fiancé. In case, she said, I copied all those other assistants and fell for you.'

Moving away, she clenched her hands.

'I needed that job so much,' she rushed on, wanting to get the worst over and end her own misery, 'I asked Thomas to co-operate, and he agreed. He's never loved me, nor I him. The ring was your aunt's. I told her Thomas couldn't afford one, which was true.'

Would Wade get up, pull on his clothes and walk out?

There was such a long silence, she decided the worst was about to happen. He intended to send her packing, right now.

'So you see,' she added tensely, 'I'm one of those impostors you said you hated.' She drew in a breath. 'If you want to leave, I'll—I'll understand. It's been g-great knowing you.'

Wade's eyes were veiled by his lashes. His hold on her body hadn't slackened. At last he spoke. 'I wondered when you were going to tell me the truth.'

Her eyes fell. 'OK, d-don't hang around for my benefit. And—and please be assured, I don't regret what's happened between us one bit.' She made to move from the bed, but he jerked her stiflingly close.

'Do you really think I didn't guess?'

'You—you knew? How long?'

'Almost from the start. I used my eyes, my ears, my intelligence. Did you honestly think I would have made love to you in the way I did if I really believed you and Thomas were serious about marriage?'

'But, Wade, the awful things you said to me about my "flexible morals", about my wanting a "fling before marriage with a newsreel idol", and that I'd read too much meaning into your kisses . . .'

'What did you expect me to say after the brutal way you rejected my lovemaking?'

'In calling out Thomas's name? But that was purely a defence mechanism on my part, because if you'd gone any further . . .'

'Hell, I wish you'd told me!'

She stroked his hair. 'Darling, did I hurt your male pride? I'm really sorry.'

Wade's teeth snapped together. 'That wasn't the only thing you hurt!' He grimaced in mock anguish and they both laughed, reaching for each other again.

It was some time later that Wade said, nuzzling her ear, 'You can tell your friend Thomas from me that, as a sham lover, he's a lousy actor. And, my love,' he took her in his arms, 'so are you. The little touches that were missing between you, the gaps in your knowledge about him . . . not to mention his neglect of you when he spent so many hours at Estée's and Jimmy's. And with Anita. All these things persuaded me that either you were unbelievably ingenuous and mistook sisterly feelings for those of love, or, for some reason I couldn't fathom, yours was a false engagement.'

Miranda settled more comfortably into his arms, watching his face as he talked. In her imagination she drew a screen around his head and pretended she was watching a television close-up. She reached out to touch him, and laughed delightedly when he nipped at her finger as it poised to press his lips.

'You,' he growled, 'can stop teasing. You haven't been seduced by a shadowy, intangible image, but the real man.'

'You can say that again!' Miranda exclaimed, nuzzling her cheek against his. 'So how did you hit upon the truth?'

'About you and Thomas? In the end, my aunt enlightened me. But not before she received her ring

from you by post. I was staying with her and she asked
me to decipher the meaning of your note.'

'That Thomas and I had no intention of getting
married?'

He nodded. 'I suspect the wording of your statement
was deliberately vague?'

Miranda nodded.

'I guessed so,' he went on. 'When she explained that
she'd taken such a liking to you, and you seemed so
intelligent,' he ruffled her hair, 'she didn't want to lose
you in the way she'd lost the others, myself being the
cause, she'd thought that employing an engaged girl as
an assistant was the best way of avoiding that situation.
Not surprisingly, I grew angry——'

'With me?'

'With my aunt for forcing the issue, and with you for
the subterfuge. However, I soon forgave you both,
especially you, for obvious reasons.'

He looked down at her and her bones threatened to
melt under the full force of the Wade Bedford smile.

'When I'd simmered down,' he continued, after a
pause, when the lips forming the famous smile had left
their mark on those of the girl in his arms, 'I told her the
truth about my feelings—that I loved you. So, with her
delight ringing, almost literally, in my ears, I drove like
crazy all the way from Scotland to London. The rest
you know. Except,' he pulled her the length of him,
letting her feel the power of his desire all mixed in with
his superior strength, 'that I have every intention of
making you my wife. Any objections?'

She sparkled up at him. 'Darling,' she answered, 'I
wouldn't dare!'

His mouth descended possessively, and it was when
the day had had a few more hours added to it that,
dressed after a shower they had shared, Miranda found
herself sprawled across him on the low armchair.

'Darling,' she whispered against his temple, 'I don't

know how I'm going to be able to stand it when you go back to your job. Seeing you on that screen again nearly killed me! The guns were firing and you were standing there, so horribly vulnerable, risking your life . . .'

'No problem,' he answered blandly. 'My contract has ended. I went back to see it out. I'd already decided to change the direction of my career.'

She flung her arms around him, and it was some time before he could continue.

'You and I are going back to working on my book. Right?' She nodded her agreement. 'The reason for Jimmy's impatience on the subject was that I'd promised to finish it to a deadline. After publication, Estée will be working on a script.'

'It's going to be made into a film?'

'A series for television.'

'Darling that's wonderful news!' Miranda took a chance on a possible mood change. 'Wade—about Thomas?'

His eyes hardened, his mouth, a mere breath from hers, firmed alarmingly. 'What about him?'

'It's only that—well, his sister Penny told me that someone's been helping him financially. Is it Jimmy, do you think? Or would it be Estée——?'

A moment's pause, then, 'Jimmy's promised him a job at the end of his course, but I'm the one who's sponsoring him, giving him guidance as well as any necessary cash.'

Miranda's head jerked back. 'Wade, why?'

'First, he's good, shows great promise. You realise that? Second,' his broad shoulders moved impatiently, 'since the woman I loved had called out his name at the most crucial, most intimate moment in our lovemaking—remember that, although I'd sussed him out as a sham fiancé, at the time I couldn't be sure of your feelings for him—I deduced that you must be madly in love with him, although it was quite plain that he didn't return it. So I decided there and then to help the man I thought the woman I loved—loved. Get it?'

Her eyes shone, her lips put tiny kisses all over his mouth. 'You're so generous, I—you've left me speechless.' She gazed into his eyes, encountering happiness mixed potently with immoderate desire. 'Will you ever forgive me, darling, for committing the dreadful sin of falling at the great Wade Bedford's feet, after all?'

'I'd never have forgiven you if you hadn't.'

'I'm your greatest fan,' she said, nuzzling up to him. 'The difference is that the others worshipped the shadow, whereas I'm head over heels in love with the substance. And,' she opened his shirt buttons and kissed every part of his chest that she could reach, 'what substance!'

His arms enfolded her and that 'substance' proceeded to take the girl in his arms back to bed and, once there, carry her with him all the way to the pinnacle of their very own, very private, pyramid-shaped mountain.

You'll flip . . . your pages won't!
Read paperbacks *hands-free* with

Book Mate • I

The perfect "mate" for all your romance paperbacks

Traveling • Vacationing • At Work • In Bed • Studying • Cooking • Eating

Perfect size for all standard paperbacks, this wonderful invention makes reading a pure pleasure! Ingenious design holds paperback books OPEN and FLAT so even wind can't ruffle pages— leaves your hands free to do other things. Reinforced, wipe-clean vinyl-covered holder flexes to let you turn pages without undoing the strap...supports paperbacks so well, they have the strength of hardcovers!

Pages turn WITHOUT opening the strap.

SEE-THROUGH STRAP

Reinforced back stays flat.

Built in bookmark

BOOK MARK

BACK COVER HOLDING STRIP

10 x 7¼ . opened Snaps closed for easy carrying. too

BM-GR

PASSPORT TO ROMANCE VACATION SWEEPSTAKES

OFFICIAL RULES

SWEEPSTAKES RULES AND REGULATIONS. NO PURCHASE NECESSARY.

HOW TO ENTER:

1. To enter, complete this official entry form and return with your invoice in the envelope provided, or print your name, address, telephone number and age on a plain piece of paper and mail to: Passport to Romance, P.O. Box #1397, Buffalo, N.Y. 14269-1397. No mechanically reproduced entries accepted.
2. All entries must be received by the Contest Closing Date, midnight, December 31, 1990 to be eligible.
3. Prizes: There will be ten (10) Grand Prizes awarded, each consisting of a choice of a trip for two people to: i) London, England (approximate retail value $5,050 U.S.); ii) England, Wales and Scotland (approximate retail value $6,400 U.S.); iii) Caribbean Cruise (approximate retail value $7,300 U.S.; iv) Hawaii (approximate retail value $ 9,550 U.S.); v) Greek Island Cruise in the Mediterranean (approximate retail value $12,250 U.S.); vi) France (approximate retail value $7,300 U.S.).
4. Any winner may choose to receive any trip or a cash alternative prize of $5,000.00 U.S. in lieu of the trip.
5. Odds of winning depend on number of entries received.
6. A random draw will be made by Nielsen Promotion Services, an independent judging organization on January 29, 1991, in Buffalo, N.Y., at 11:30 a.m. from all eligible entries received on or before the Contest Closing Date. Any Canadian entrants who are selected must correctly answer a time-limited, mathematical skill-testing question in order to win. Quebec residents may submit any litigation respecting the conduct and awarding of a prize in this contest to the Régie des loteries et courses du Quebec.
7. Full contest rules may be obtained by sending a stamped, self-addressed envelope to: "Passport to Romance Rules Request", P.O. Box 9998, Saint John, New Brunswick, E2L 4N4.
8. Payment of taxes other than air and hotel taxes is the sole responsibility of the winner.
9. Void where prohibited by law.

PASSPORT TO ROMANCE VACATION SWEEPSTAKES

OFFICIAL RULES

SWEEPSTAKES RULES AND REGULATIONS. NO PURCHASE NECESSARY.

HOW TO ENTER:

1. To enter, complete this official entry form and return with your invoice in the envelope provided, or print your name, address, telephone number and age on a plain piece of paper and mail to: Passport to Romance, P.O. Box #1397, Buffalo, N.Y. 14269-1397. No mechanically reproduced entries accepted.
2. All entries must be received by the Contest Closing Date, midnight, December 31, 1990 to be eligible.
3. Prizes: There will be ten (10) Grand Prizes awarded, each consisting of a choice of a trip for two people to: i) London, England (approximate retail value $5,050 U.S.); ii) England, Wales and Scotland (approximate retail value $6,400 U.S.); iii) Caribbean Cruise (approximate retail value $7,300 U.S.; iv) Hawaii (approximate retail value $ 9,550 U.S.); **v)** Greek Island Cruise in the Mediterranean (approximate retail value $12,250 U.S.); vi) France (approximate retail value $7,300 U.S.).
4. Any winner may choose to receive any **trip** or a cash alternative prize of $5,000.00 U.S. in lieu of the trip.
5. Odds of winning depend on number of entries received.
6. A random draw will be made by Nielsen Promotion Services, an independent judging organization on January 29, 1991, in Buffalo, N.Y., at 11:30 a.m. from all eligible entries received on or before the Contest Closing Date. Any Canadian entrants who are selected must correctly answer a time-limited, mathematical skill-testing question in order to win. Quebec residents may submit any litigation respecting the conduct and awarding of a prize in this contest to the Régie des loteries et courses du Quebec.
7. Full contest rules may be obtained by sending a stamped, self-addressed envelope to: "Passport to Romance Rules Request", P.O. Box 9998, Saint John, New Brunswick, E2L 4N4.
8. Payment of taxes other than air and hotel taxes is the sole responsibility of the winner.
9. Void where prohibited by law.

PASSPORT TO ROMANCE
WIN 1 of 10 Vacations
SEE INSIDE

VACATION SWEEPSTAKES

MONTH 3 ENTRY

Official Entry Form

Yes, enter me in the drawing for one of ten Vacations-for-Two! If I'm a winner, I'll get my choice of any of the six different destinations being offered — and I won't have to decide until after I'm notified!

Return entries with invoice in envelope provided along with Daily Travel Allowance Voucher. Each book in your shipment has two entry forms — and the more you enter, the better your chance of winning!

Name

Address _____ Apt.

City _____ State/Prov. _____ Zip/Postal Code

Daytime phone number _____
                        Area Code

☐ I am enclosing a Daily Travel Allowance Voucher in the amount of $_____ Write in amount revealed beneath scratch-off

CPS-THREE